Elizabeth Gail and the Great Canoe Conspiracy

Hilda Stahl

Tyndale House Publishers, Inc. Wheaton, Illinois

Dedicated with love to Sonya Lorraine McNeely

Cover illustration copyright © 1991 by David F. Henderson
Interior illustration copyright © 1990 by Kathy Kulin Sandel

Library of Congress Catalog Card Number 90-90365
ISBN 0-8423-0815-6
Copyright © 1991 by Word Spinners, Inc.
Printed in the United States of America

98 97 96 95 94 93
9   8   7   6   5   4

Dear Reader:
Congratulations! You're about to go on a whole
new adventure with Elizabeth Gail and her
friends and family! Because this is an all new
adventure, it is book number 19. But the story
actually takes place right after book #4, Eliza-
beth Gail and the Dangerous Double.

We hope you will enjoy reading about Eliza-
beth Gail and her great adventures. (A complete
list of the exciting Elizabeth Gail books follows.)
And keep your eyes open for more brand-new
Elizabeth Gail books coming soon!

The Elizabeth Gail Series

Contents

ONE
The terrible dream

Libby plunked the piano keys as she glared toward
the family room door. She could hear Chuck and
Susan laughing as they walked past. Libby narrowed
her hazel eyes. How dare Susan take all of Chuck's
time! "Dad!" Libby called.

Chuck poked his head in the doorway. His face
was flushed with laughter and looked almost as
red as his hair. "Did you call me, Elizabeth?" He
always called her by her full name instead of her
nickname.

She managed a smile. "Can you listen to me prac-
tice my new song now?"

He shook his head. "Sorry, Elizabeth, but I promised Susan I'd play ping-pong with her."

Libby sat very still, a half-smile glued on her face.

Just then Susan peeked around Chuck's arm,
her red-gold ponytails bobbing over her ears. She giggled. "He thinks he can beat me, Libby. But he can't!"

"Says who?" Chuck pulled her close and knuckled
the top of her bright head. "See you later, Elizabeth.

I got one smart daughter who thinks she can beat her old dad."

Tears burned Libby's eyes and she ducked her head as Chuck and Susan ran to the basement for their

game. "He loves Susan more than me," Libby whispered hoarsely. But why shouldn't he? Susan, Ben, and Kevin were the real Johnson children. Toby was adopted, but she was still just a foster kid—or an aid kid, as some people called her. Libby's real mother wouldn't sign the paper to give the Johnsons permission to adopt her. Mother said she'd never sign the paper. Libby shivered.

"I won't think about *her*," Libby said as she brought her hands down hard on the piano keys. The noise rang across the family room and out into the hall. She knew Chuck and Susan wouldn't hear the noise over their laughter. Vera and the boys were outside having too much fun playing softball to notice her. Why was everyone having a good time while she was practicing piano? They wouldn't care! They were probably glad she wasn't outside with them—that way they didn't have to watch her strike out.

Warm wind blew in the open window. A rooster crowed and Rex barked. Libby glanced out the window. Goosy Poosy was probably playing first base with Kevin. The big white goose still liked to chase Libby when she walked in the yard alone. The first day Miss Miller brought Libby to the Johnson farm Goosy Poosy had flown toward her and knocked her to the ground. Since then, she'd been terrified of him. But this morning before going to Sunday school Kevin dared her to touch the goose. She had a hard time finding the courage, but she soon felt brave enough to pet Goosy Poosy. Chuck had seen what she'd done and he was proud of her for getting over her fear of the goose.

She bit her lower lip. The aroma of the lilacs on the

table beside the sofa filled the room. She rubbed her hands down her jeans and swung her feet under the piano bench. Tears burned her eyes and she sniffed.

Chuck had loved her so much when she'd first come to live with the Johnson family in November. Had she done something terrible to make him hate her? Hadn't petting Goosy Poosy helped after all?

Libby wiped a tear away. She knew Chuck really didn't hate her. Chuck was a Christian and she knew Jesus wanted Christians to love one another. So, Chuck didn't hate her; he just didn't love her. Maybe it was because she was tall, thin, and ugly and not at all pretty, short, and giggly like Susan.

"I hate her," mouthed Libby, then clapped her hand over her mouth and shook her head. It was wrong to hate, but she couldn't help herself. Right now she felt as though she hated Susan more than she hated Brenda Wilkens, the neighbor girl who always caused problems for her. Just thinking about hating Susan made Libby shudder.

"No! No, I don't hate Susan!"

Libby jumped up and ran to the window, and looked out across the yard. There was a large tree near by, and a wide swing hung from a fat branch that was just leafing out. The grass was all worn away under the swing, but the rest of the lawn was green and beautifully mowed. Libby and Susan had mowed it yesterday when they'd still been friends.

With a strangled sob, Libby ran into the hall upstairs. The smell of the chocolate cake that Ben had baked before the ball game still hung in the air. Libby stumbled on the top step and grabbed the smooth banister before she tumbled back down the stairs. If Chuck knew how she felt about Susan he'd be very disappointed in her. What if he gave up on her and sent her back to Social Services? Once again she'd be sent to live with new foster parents. None of the other foster parents had cared for her as well as the Johnsons had. But maybe even the Johnsons didn't care now.

If Chuck really loved her, he would've sat down and listened to the new song she'd learned, wouldn't he? He would've knuckled her head and teased her instead of Susan.

Libby ran into her bedroom, flung herself across the bed and buried her face in Pinky's soft fur. Susan had given her the big pink stuffed dog for her bed when she'd first come. Impatiently, Libby flung Pinky to the floor and hugged Teddy, her bear.

But even hugging Teddy didn't help make her feel better. Probably nothing would.

Several minutes later Susan danced into the room, giggling happily. "I beat him, Libby. I said I would win and I did!"

Libby shot up from the bed and Susan jumped back in alarm. "Who said you could come in here?" Libby demanded angrily.

"Libby? What's wrong?" Susan's blue eyes clouded over.

Libby shook her finger at Susan. "I don't want you in my room!"

Susan bumped against the large red hassock. "But we were going to plan what to do together tomorrow for Activity Day."

Libby tugged her blue sweatshirt down over her jeans. "You do what you want and I'll do what I want!"

Susan bit her bottom lip and then said, "I'm signed up to go canoeing with Gabby and Nedra, but I don't have plans for the rest of the time."

"Just do everything without me! See if I care!" Libby flipped back her mousy brown hair and glared at Susan.

Susan backed away, but then lifted her chin and glared back at Libby. "If you're going to be such a brat then I'll just leave. You can find someone else to be partners with tomorrow. Or you can go alone all day long!" She spun around and ran out, slamming the door behind her.

"There!" said Libby, brushing her hands together. Her stomach knotted painfully, but she ignored it.

After eating supper and completing her nighttime chores, Libby took a shower and dressed in her cool pink pajamas. A warm breeze blew her pink curtains away from the window. She sat at her desk and looked at the puzzle box that her real dad had sent to her. She touched her Bible, but then pulled her hand away. *I don't have time to read tonight,* she thought to herself. *I'm tired and need lots of sleep for tomorrow's dumb Activity Day.* She turned away from her Bible. She'd be glad when school was out for the summer. Next week the family was going to Camp Talease, the church camp, a new experience for Libby. Maybe Chuck would have more time for her there. Later in June they were going to visit Sandhill Ranch in Nebraska. She touched the puzzle box again. Her real dad had given her his share of Sandhill Ranch. Finally she'd get to see it. But did she want to see it? Did she even want to go to Nebraska? Maybe she wouldn't have a choice.

14

Impatiently she jumped up. She might not get to go to Camp Talease or to the Sandhill Ranch. Maybe she'd be in another foster home. Or even worse—her stomach tightened—the court could send her back to Mother.

"No!" she whispered in agony and shook her head.

There was a timid knock at the door. Libby froze.

"Libby, it's Susan. May I come in?"

Libby swallowed hard, then slowly opened the door. Susan looked like she was ready to cry. "What do you want, Susan?"

"I don't want to go to bed mad at you, Libby. I'm sorry for losing my temper. Please forgive me."

Libby shrugged.

Susan twisted the ruffle on her lilac pajama top. "Aren't you sorry for being mean to me?"

"No!"

"Well, you should be!"

"I'm not!" Libby slammed the door in Susan's face, clicked off the light, and slipped between the sheets. She really was sorry, but not sorry enough to say so. Susan always got everything she wanted, but not this time!

The door opened and Libby sat bolt upright, ready to tell Susan to get out. But instead of Susan, she found Chuck and Vera standing there, smiling.

"We came to say good night," said Vera as she brushed a strand of blonde hair off her cheek.

"Sleep well," said Chuck. They kissed Libby's cheek, but didn't stay and talk like they usually did. Instead, they walked out hand in hand, talking about the bookwork Chuck had to do for his store.

Libby sank back against her pillow and looked at

the partly closed door. "If he really loved me as much as he did before, he would've asked me what was wrong," she whispered.

Susan's laughter rang down the hall and Libby's jaw tightened.

"It's all *her* fault!" Libby muttered. "Oh, I wish something really, really bad would happen to her!"

Libby locked her fingers under her head and stared up at the ceiling. Maybe Susan would turn mean and ugly during the night so that the whole family would stop loving her.

The smell of bubble bath drifted from the bathroom into Libby's bedroom. Ben's voice rumbled as he talked to Kevin and Toby. After a long time the house grew quiet and Libby flipped on her side and tried to sleep. She closed her eyes and sank deep into her pillow.

Suddenly Libby was grabbing Susan and dragging her by her gorgeous three-foot long ponytails along a trail through the woods.

"Don't do this to me, Libby!" cried Susan. "We're sisters!"

"No, we're not! I'm Libby Dobbs and you're Susan Johnson!"

All of a sudden, they were in a house, a terrible house that Libby had been in before. She pushed Susan in an empty closet and locked the door. "Now stay there until you can be good!" snapped Libby.

"Let me out! Please, let me out!" shouted Susan as she pounded on the door, but Libby just walked away.

In a flash Libby was the one inside the locked closet, pounding on the door. Susan was gone; it was as if she never existed. Libby pounded harder on the

door. "Mother! Mother, let me out! Don't lock me in again! Please! Mother!"

"You stop that yelling, Libby!" cried Mother from the other side of the door. "You've been a bad girl and you will stay in there until you can be good!"

"Mother!" Libby knocked so hard that her fists hurt as much as her stomach did. Finally, she sank to the floor and sobbed into her trembling hands.

Suddenly Libby jerked up in bed, her face wet with tears and her skin damp with perspiration. A soft light shone from the hallway. She touched her bed and looked at the room that had become so familiar to her. She wasn't locked in a closet the way she had been many times in the past when she'd lived with Mother. It had been a dream—a terrible, terrible dream. She was safe in her own bed at the Johnsons' farm.

But *was* she really safe here? Would the Johnsons stop loving her, maybe even start to dislike her, and then send her away to live in another foster home?

With a moan, Libby curled into a tight ball and sobbed into her pillow.

TWO
Monday morning

With her back to Susan, Libby spread peanut butter
over a slice of wheat bread, then globbed grape jelly
on the other slice of her sandwich. A knot bigger than
the knot in Toby's shoelace tightened in her stomach.
She probably wouldn't even want to eat lunch, but
she had to fix it or Vera would question her. She
crammed her sandwich in a plastic bag as the others
talked around her. Libby pulled her sweat-shirt over
her jeans and leaned against the counter.

How could Chuck leave this morning without even
saying good-bye to her? It was the very first time he'd
ever done that since she'd moved in. But she had
taken too long to feed the horses and see that the
sheep had water. She frowned. He still should've said
good-bye.

"We're going to have so much fun today!" said Susan,
twirling around the large kitchen. Bright morning
sunlight streamed in the windows. Smells of eggs,
bacon, and toast hung in the air. "I love going to
Pontiac State Park! You'll have a lot of fun, too, Libby."

Libby checked to make sure Vera wasn't looking, then stuck her tongue out at Susan. Susan frowned and turned quickly away to finish packing her lunch.

"Toby, I don't know how you could get your shoelace in such a knot," said Vera as she carefully picked away at the knot with a fork.

"I don't know either," Toby said. His face and neck turned as red as his hair. He started to stick his thumb in his mouth, but stopped himself and just tucked it behind him. He'd been trying to stop sucking his thumb since the Johnsons had adopted him a few months ago. He looked closer at the knot. "I tried for a long time to get it out, but I couldn't."

"I don't know if I can, either," said Vera impatiently. She brushed back her blonde hair and dropped down on a kitchen chair. Sighing, she rubbed her hands down her jeans and bent over the knot again.

"Want me to try?" asked Ben. At twelve years old he was the oldest, and he thought he could do anything. Usually he could. His hair was a darker red than Toby's, but since they both had red hair and freckles they looked enough alike to be natural brothers.

"I think I've got it now," said Vera with one last tug with the fork. The knot fell apart and Vera smiled in triumph. "There you go, Toby."

"Thanks," said Toby as he sat on the floor and put on his sneaker.

Kevin opened the refrigerator and peered inside. He pushed his glasses up on his round face and brushed his baby-fine blonde hair off his wide forehead. "What else can I take for lunch, Mom?" This ten-year-old was always hungry.

"You can have my apple," said Libby, holding it out
to him. He reached for it, but Vera stopped him.

"Libby, you have to have a piece of fruit," said Vera.
"Kevin, open the vegetable bin and you'll find apples
and oranges. Take two of each if you want." Vera
opened a drawer and pulled out a pack of chocolate
candy bars. "You can each take one of these, too, if
you want."

Libby dropped one in her lunch bag with her sandwich and apple. The school was providing cans of pop
for everyone, so she didn't have to carry a drink with
her. Oh, how she wanted to run upstairs and hide under the covers!

"We could hike together, Libby," said Susan. It was
already her fourth suggestion, but Libby had turned
down each one.

Libby wanted to snap at Susan, but she didn't dare
with Vera standing right beside them. Vera insisted
they speak kindly to each other. "I don't really want
to hike," said Libby as she turned away from the hurt
look on Susan's face.

"I hear the bus honking at the Wilkens!" cried Ben,
grabbing his sack lunch and heading for the door.
"See you later, Mom."

"Bye, Ben. Bye, kids," said Vera, making sure that
Kevin and Toby didn't forget anything as they hur-
ried out the door.

Goosy Poosy honked from the chicken pen. Apache
Girl whinnied from the pen beside the horse barn.
Many of the lilac bushes were still in bloom and the
aroma filled the air.

The sun felt warm against Libby as she raced
after Ben. She could run almost as fast as he could

and a lot faster than Susan. Libby wanted to find a seat where Susan couldn't sit beside her. She didn't want to hear about all the things they could do together.

Libby stopped at the front of the aisle and looked for a place to sit. She could smell the kids' lunches, as well as somebody's stinky sneakers. She saw a spot beside Brenda Wilkens, but there was no way she'd sit there.

"Hey, Aid Kid!" called Brenda with a sneer. "I hope you get lost today at Pontiac State Park."

"I hope a kindergarten kid throws up all over you!" snapped Libby as she walked past Brenda's seat.

Susan jabbed Libby in the back. "Stop that, Libby," she whispered. "You're supposed to be nice. You know Jesus said to be kind to others."

Libby did know that, and she really did want to be kind, but she was hurt because she was sure Chuck didn't love her. She reached around and yanked one of Susan's ponytails. "I can act however I want and you can't stop me. So there!"

Susan's lip trembled, but she didn't cry. She took a seat beside a first grader.

Libby found an empty seat and huddled against the window. She knew before they reached town that someone would have to sit there. She peeked at Susan, but her head was down, her red-gold hair shielding her pretty face. Libby looked quickly away.

Just then Ben leaned up from where he sat behind Libby and whispered, "What's wrong, Elizabeth?"

His breath tickled her neck and his kind voice almost brought tears to her eyes, but she forced them back and just shrugged. If she tried to tell him how she felt she knew she'd burst into tears. Then Brenda Wilkens would really tease her.

"Don't be afraid about Activity Day," he said. "You'll have fun."

She nodded. Ben was almost always nice to her. He'd taught her to ride a horse, do the chores, and play ping-pong. She told him what frightened her and he always helped her. New things like Activity Day did scare her some, but today she was too angry at Susan and too hurt to think about being afraid.

Finally Ben leaned back in his seat and Libby breathed easier. It was hard to stay angry with Ben around.

Later Libby stepped off the bus to find Susan waiting for her. Boys and girls swarmed off the line of buses, laughing and shouting.

"Please, Libby," said Susan softly. "I don't want you to be mad at me. I want to do something with you today."

Libby's heart softened and she opened her mouth to say she would do something with Susan after all.

Just then Susan cried, "Look! There's Dad!"

Susan ran toward Chuck's pickup, but before Libby could move, Brenda Wilkens grabbed her lunch and tossed it into a bush beside the sidewalk.

As Brenda laughed and walked on, Libby glared at her and then ran for her lunch. She grabbed it and raced toward Susan and Chuck. She saw him bend down and kiss Susan's cheek, then climb into the pickup.

"Dad!" called Libby, waving hard.

Chuck smiled and waved and drove off. Libby's heart sank and her shoulders drooped. How she wanted to have him pull her close and tell her how much he loved her!

"He brought our permission slips for today," said Susan. "Mom forgot to give them to us this morning."

"Why didn't he wait and give me mine?" asked Libby in a weak voice.

"He had to get back to the store," said Susan. She held one slip out to Libby and pushed the other in the pocket of her jeans. Chuck owned the general store in town and he often worked long hours.

Slowly Libby pushed the paper in the pocket of her jeans, then turned away and walked toward the group of sixth graders near the band room. Chuck had taken time to talk to Susan and even kiss her cheek. Hot tears burned Libby's eyes. Why didn't he have time for her anymore?

"Wait, Libby," said Susan, walking beside her. "Let's eat lunch together today if we can't do anything else."

Libby whirled around and hissed, "No! Now, leave me alone!" She saw the pain on Susan's face but she didn't care. Susan deserved all the pain she could give her!

Susan walked slowly toward two of her friends and Libby walked to a group of girls who were talking and laughing. Libby tried to talk with them, but they acted as if she wasn't there. Even though her jeans, sweatshirt, and sneakers were nice, and her hair was combed neatly, she knew the girls still remembered she was a foster kid who had been in school only since November.

Slowly, with a heavy heart, Libby walked away to see if another group would let her join in, but none would. Some of them were nice to her, but none of them wanted to take time for her.

She frowned. Activity Day was a dumb idea. Who wanted to go to Pontiac State Park anyway?

The sixth-grade boys and girls laughed and shouted. They seemed excited about the day. A gentle breeze blew enough to keep the sun from feeling too hot. The kids who weren't going to Pontiac State Park ran into the school. The sixth-grade teachers and parents who had volunteered to help for the day stood in a group talking. Some of them looked excited, others bored or anxious. None of them glanced Libby's way.

She looked around for Susan and finally saw her with several girls. She was laughing at something Jamie Smith had said. Libby gripped her lunch bag so tight it almost ripped.

Somehow she'd find a way to make Susan sorry that she was short and pretty and loved best by Chuck.

THREE
The terrible plan

Libby crept behind a bush, sat on the grass, and leaned against the brick wall of the school. She could smell her peanut butter and jelly sandwich. A small hunger pang hit her for an instant, but then disappeared. She hadn't been able to force all her breakfast down this morning after she'd realized Chuck had left without saying good-bye.

Just then, two girls stopped a short distance from Libby. She knew they couldn't see her, but she could see them. It was Gabby and Nedra, the girls Susan was going canoeing with at Pontiac State Park. They were talking in hushed voices, but Libby could still hear them clearly.

"I tried to get Susan to sign up with two others," said Gabby angrily. "But she wouldn't! Can you believe it? She said she wanted to go with us."

"You'd think she'd know when she's not wanted," snapped Nedra.

"She thinks everybody likes her just because she likes everybody," said Gabby. She chewed her gum harder. "She's so goody-goody she makes me sick!"

"I told Jenny I'd get rid of Susan so she could go with us, but I couldn't," said Nedra with a loud sigh. "And Jenny almost stayed home today because of it! Susan makes me so mad!"

Libby nodded in agreement. It made her feel strange to eavesdrop on the girls, but she sat very still so she could hear more. She was glad Gabby and Nedra agreed with her about Susan.

Suddenly Gabby clapped and giggled. "I just thought of a plan to get rid of Susan!" she said. "This is *so* good!"

"So, what is it?" asked Nedra with a giggle. "Hurry and tell me before someone walks over and hears you."

Libby stiffened. Were they going to hurt Susan?

"I've been to Pontiac State Park a lot of times," said Gabby, her voice full of excitement. "There are lots of islands in the lake where we'll go canoeing."

"And?" asked Nedra breathlessly.

Libby strained to hear. She couldn't miss the plan now.

Gabby giggled. "We'll paddle out to the island that's close to one end of the lake, and we'll say we're going to get out and look around the island."

"And? And?"

Sweat broke out on Libby's forehead and upper lip. Her heart beat so loud she was afraid the girls could hear it.

"And when Susan is out of the canoe and on the island, we'll paddle away and leave her!"

Libby bit back a gasp. How could the girls be that

mean to Susan? Then Libby frowned. What was she thinking? She was glad they were being mean to Susan!

Nedra let out her breath. "Oh, Gabby! Do you really think we should do that?"

"Yes!"

Libby swallowed hard.

"But she'd be stranded there!" cried Nedra.

"So? Somebody would find her after a while," said Gabby with a laugh.

"That's true," said Nedra.

Libby wanted to jump up and tell the girls she'd heard everything, but she didn't move.

"So, shall we do it?" asked Gabby with a breathless laugh.

"Yes!" cried Nedra. "But we won't tell anybody else except Jenny. We don't want Susan to hear a word about our wonderful plan."

The girls walked away, giggling.

Her eyes wide, Libby bit her bottom lip. She had to find Susan and tell her not to go with Nedra and Gabby!

Libby peeked around the bush to make sure the girls were indeed gone, then scrambled out. She pulled a twig from her shoulder-length brown hair and brushed the back of her jeans off. She looked around for Susan and spotted her talking to two of the parents. They were looking at Susan as if she were a princess on a throne. Libby took a step forward, then stopped.

"Why should I tell her?" whispered Libby through her suddenly dry throat. "It would serve Susan right to be stranded on an island with no way off!"

Just then Susan turned and spotted Libby. Susan waved and ran to Libby's side. Libby wanted to sink through the ground, but she didn't move. She stared down at Susan's white sneakers.

"I just found out they're going to have a three-legged race this afternoon, Libby," said Susan with a breathless laugh. "Oh, please, please, be my partner! Please! We've run them at home, so we know we're good at it."

Libby started to tell Susan she would not ever run another three-legged race with her, then stopped. Susan would be stranded on an island by then anyway, so why not tell her what she wanted to hear? Libby grinned wickedly. "Sure, Susan. I'll race with you."

"You will? Great!" Susan laughed and squeezed Libby's arm. "You're the best sister in the whole world!"

Guilt rose inside Libby and she had to look away from Susan so she wouldn't tell her of Gabby's and Nedra's plans.

Just then Miss Keene called the sixth graders to attention. Thankfully Libby ran with Susan to stand in two long lines with the other sixth graders.

Mr. Everson held up his hand for silence. When everyone was quiet he said, "We're going to use the buddy system today. That means each of you will have a partner to keep track of all day long. So, as quietly as you can, find a partner."

Libby slipped away before Susan could choose her. Before Libby realized it, everyone she knew had a partner.

"Is there anyone without a partner?" shouted Mrs. Franks.

Reluctantly Libby raised her hand. She looked around and saw only one other person without a partner. It was Clay Barett, the boy who sniffed all the time. The boy nobody liked. He saw her look of dismay and he scowled. She knew he didn't want to be her partner any more than she wanted to be his.

"Clay and Libby, you're partners," said Mrs. Franks, jotting the names on her clipboard.

Slowly Libby walked toward him and he walked toward her. They each carried a sack lunch and he carried a red backpack. They stood side by side and waited for Mr. Everson to tell the rules. Libby felt as if she towered over Clay. He hiked up his new jeans, pulled his gray T-shirt down, and sniffed.

She glared down at him. He looked up at her and sniffed again. She turned away in disgust.

"Got a boyfriend, Libby?" called Tina Greggory, one of Brenda Wilkens' friends.

Libby clamped her mouth shut and didn't answer. She was glad Brenda was in seventh grade and couldn't go on the field trip. Tina Greggory would be bad enough.

A few minutes later Libby walked in front of Clay up onto the bus. They had to sit together on the bus and know where each other was all day long. Libby found a seat close to the front so she wouldn't have to walk past the others and listen to their teasing remarks. Clay sat beside her and sniffed. He had light brown eyes and neatly cut light brown hair.

Libby watched Susan and her partner Jamie Smith talking and laughing as they walked in line to board the bus. Libby looked around until she found Gabby and Nedra. They were only three seats back from her.

They were whispering with their heads close together. Libby smiled mischievously. Maybe they were talking about the plans for Susan.

Voices buzzed around Libby and smells of all kinds filled the bus. She opened the window as far as she was allowed and tried to breathe in fresh air. Gas and oil fumes from the other buses drifted in.

Just then, a honey bee buzzed through the window and landed on her hand. She shrieked, but sat frozen in fright.

Clay lifted her hand by her wrist and flicked the bee back out the window. Without a word he sat back down. He sniffed.

She peeked at him from the corner of her eye, but she didn't say a word.

"Clay saved your life, Libby," called Timmy Oltz with a loud laugh. "He's your hero now."

"Heroes always get kissed," said Alison Jones, giggling. "Give him a big kiss, Libby Dobbs!"

Libby's face turned brick red. She clenched her hands over her lunch and stared down at her bony knees.

"Libby and Clay, love forever!" shouted several of the kids.

A scream rose in Libby's throat and she started to jump up to tell the kids just what she thought of them, but Clay grasped her arm with a surprisingly strong grip and held her down. She glared at him and saw him barely shake his head. Trembling, she turned to look out the window again. Finally he let go of her arm. She didn't jump up.

The bus doors closed and the bus started out with a jerk. In less than an hour they would be at Pontiac State Park.

Clay opened his backpack, pulled out a small video game and started playing it. The tiny beeps seemed to hammer against Libby's head.

She leaned her head back and closed her eyes. This was going to be a very long day. The only good thing about it would be Susan getting stranded on an island.

Clay sniffed, blew his nose, and sniffed again.

Libby wanted to ask him what in the world his problem was, but he had saved her from the bee and from making a laughingstock of herself in front of the others, so she kept her mouth locked shut.

The beeping suddenly stopped. "All right!" said Clay just above a whisper.

Libby looked at Clay through her lashes as he smiled down at his game and started over.

FOUR
Pontiac State Park

Libby kicked a clump of dirt and watched it
skid across the path that led to the pond. All of the
sixth graders seemed to be talking at once as they
got ready for the first event of the morning. Clay
stood quietly beside her, just waiting, and often
sniffing.

"You can stick your lunch in my pack if you want,"
he said, slipping it off his back to slide it around
where he could open it.

"I can carry it," Libby said stiffly.

"Sure you can, but why should you? Put it in here
and your hands will be free while you're hiking."

With a scowl she stuffed the bag in his red pack
and he flipped it back in place. "Who says we're going
on a hike?" she asked sharply.

"All of the students that don't have their schedules
figured out have to go on a hike. Mr. Everson said so."

"Oh."

"We can go off by ourselves or we can stay with the
crowd." He motioned toward the group of students

led by Mrs. Zeneth, one of the volunteer parents. "Either way is okay by me."

"I don't care either," Libby said, pushing her hands deep into the pockets of her jeans. She looked around for Susan, but didn't see her. Nor could she find Nedra and Gabby. A chill ran down Libby's spine. Were they already in the canoe heading for the island? She shook her head slightly. Nobody would really follow through with such a terrible plan. It had been fun to think about for a while, but Nedra and Gabby wouldn't really leave Susan stranded. Would they?

"I know the trail," said Clay. "Besides, it's clearly marked so nobody can get lost. So, let's go by ourselves. We can see a lot more that way. We might even see a snake."

She shivered. All her life she'd lived in the city until she moved to the Johnson farm. "I don't like snakes," she said, turning away from Clay.

"I do."

She turned around and frowned down at him. "Why?"

He shrugged. "I just do."

"You're really weird."

"I know."

She saw pain flicker in his eyes, then disappear. For a minute she felt sorry for calling him weird, then shrugged the feeling away. "Are you going or not?" she asked sharply.

He stuck out his chin, squared his shoulders, and without a word strode toward the trail that led through the woods.

Libby hesitated, then walked after him, her long legs making it easy for her to catch up. She walked

beside him without speaking. The woodchip trail felt
rough under her feet. She smelled the pines and
decaying leaves. A blue jay scolded them from the
branch of a poplar tree. Wind rustled the leaves.
Soon all of the sounds were covered by the shouts
from the group of sixth graders starting on the trail
behind them.

Libby saw Clay stop to study the animal tracks in
the soft earth next to the trail, but she kept walking.

He ran to catch up with her. "Raccoon tracks," he
said. "Deer tracks, too."

She clamped her mouth shut and kept walking.
Often she saw white-tailed deer at the Johnson farm.
Clay would probably like to hear about the deer, but
she didn't tell him.

"Libby and Clay! Love forever!" shouted several of
the kids behind them.

Libby's face flamed, but she pretended she hadn't
heard. She peeked sideways at Clay, but he acted as
if the teasing didn't bother him at all. Well, if it didn't
bother him, she sure wouldn't let it bother her; "Libby
and Clay! Libby and Clay! True love!" shouted the
kids in sing-song voices.

Suddenly Clay caught Libby's arm and pulled her
to the side of the path and pointed down at the
ground. All she saw was a pile of dead oak leaves.

"What?" she asked.

"Nothing," he whispered, "but just keep looking and
watch this."

She peered closer and tried to act as if she was
studying a pile of jewels. What was he up to?

As the others reached them, Clay shouted, "Snake!
Come look at the snake!"

Several girls screamed and ran while some of the boys looked. "Where?" they asked.

"You're too late," said Clay with a shrug.

The boys walked on, then ran to catch up to the girls.

With her brow cocked questioningly, Libby looked at Clay. "Why did you do that?"

He grinned. "I figured if they're ahead of us they'll forget about teasing us."

A slow smile spread across Libby's face. "You're pretty smart."

"I've had to learn how to handle kids who tease me," he said with a shrug and a sniff.

She nodded. She'd had to learn to handle them, too. She used to just punch their lights out, but since she'd accepted Jesus as her personal Savior, she had to stop that. It had been very hard and sometimes she still forgot, just like she'd forgotten that being jealous and mean were wrong. She abruptly pushed that thought away.

Clay picked up a pinecone and tossed it into the woods. The gentle sound of its landing filtered through the trees. "I'm hungry," said Clay.

"We could share my candy bar," said Libby.

Clay found her lunch bag and handed it to her. She dug out the candy bar, opened it and broke it in half. She gave a piece to Clay, stuffed the wrapper back in her bag, and then put the bag back in his pack.

"Thanks," he said. "I usually don't eat chocolate. Mom says I'm allergic to it, but it doesn't make my nose run like dust and mold."

"Is that why you sniff all the time?"

"Yes. It's disgusting, but I can't help it." He wolfed his half of candy down in two bites.

Libby ate hers slowly, savoring the taste of melted chocolate on her tongue. "You can eat half my sandwich now if you want," she said.

"Thanks, but you'd better save it for lunch." Clay watched three goldfinches flit through the brush. "I know the names of most of the birds in our area. Mom and I learned them together once when my dad was away on a business trip. My dad was pretty impressed." Clay smiled as if he could still hear his dad's praise.

Libby frowned, thinking about Chuck. Once he would've been proud of her if she learned the names of birds, but he probably wouldn't notice now. Tears burned her eyes. She turned away from Clay and gulped great breaths of air until all the terrible tears were forced back.

Why didn't anyone love her? What was wrong with her? She knew she was tall, thin, and ugly, but was that enough of a reason? She'd seen other ugly kids with dads who loved them. Clay sniffed all the time, and his dad still loved him.

"What's wrong?" asked Clay.

She shook her head and walked away from him. She didn't stop until she was off the trail and in the recreation area with the other sixth graders. They all seemed happy about the first activities they'd done.

Just then Libby spotted Nedra and Gabby. She looked around for Susan, expecting to see her, but she couldn't find her. Fear shot through Libby. If she'd really and truly believed that Nedra and Gabby would have gone through with their plan, she would've stopped them. She would have protected Susan, wouldn't she? She flushed with guilt, suddenly unable to answer her own question. Frantically she ran from group to group. Everyone was supposed to be here now to start the next activity. But Susan wasn't here!

Libby ran to Jamie Smith. "Where's Susan?" Libby asked hoarsely, her legs weak and shaky.

Jamie shrugged. "Still on her canoe ride, I guess."

"You're her partner and you're supposed to know!" hissed Libby with her face down close to Jamie's.

"What's wrong with you, Libby? Susan will find me as soon as she's back. She said she would." Jamie frowned at Libby and walked away to talk to a friend of hers.

Libby clenched her fists as she walked around the groups of boys and girls again. Gabby and Nedra wouldn't really leave Susan on an island, would they? They were just saying they would to show off to each other. Weren't they?

Libby stopped beside Nedra and Gabby who were whispering with Jenny. "Nedra. Gabby," said Libby with a lump in her throat.

The girls looked up and gasped. They looked very guilty. "What do you want?" snapped Gabby.

"I'm looking for Susan," said Libby weakly.

Gabby shrugged. "I don't know where she is. Go ask her partner."

"Did she go canoeing with you?" asked Libby, her mouth dry.

"What if she did?" asked Nedra, her face red.

Jenny giggled, then held it back, but her shoulders continued to shake with silent laughter.

Libby whirled away and ran frantically toward Mr. Everson. She'd tell him and he'd take care of it. But then she'd have to admit that she'd known what the girls were planning to do and hadn't told anyone or tried to stop them.

Just then she spotted Clay standing alone as usual near the footbridge that led across a small creek. He'd know what to do. He'd help her. She ran to him, her face hot and her breathing ragged.

He looked up and his eyes widened in alarm. "What's wrong?" he asked.

"It's Susan," Libby said, gasping. As quickly as she could she told Clay what she'd overheard about the plan and that Susan never came back from canoeing.

"Let's go get her," he said. "We'll sign out a canoe and get her and bring her back."

"Thank you, Clay! Thank you!" As she looked at him he suddenly seemed eight feet tall. He looked so confident that she knew she could trust him to help.

"Let's go," he said, running across the footbridge.

She ran after him, her sneakers thudding on the wooden bridge.

He stopped at the canoe rental and signed their names for a canoe, slipped on a life jacket, then eased the canoe out in the blue-green water.

Butterflies fluttered in Libby's stomach. She'd only been in a canoe once in her life. She snapped the bright orange life jacket in place with trembling fingers and carefully climbed in the canoe. It swayed and she gripped the sides for dear life.

"I'm not a good swimmer," she said weakly.

"Don't worry, you're wearing a life jacket," said Clay calmly. "Just relax. I'll paddle and we'll check out the island and see if Susan really is stranded there."

"I hope she's not," said Libby. But if she was, it was her fault. Jealousy is such a terrible thing!

Clay dipped the paddle in the water and the canoe shot forward just the way he'd planned.

Libby looked at him in surprise.

"Dad taught me," he said.

"I'm glad of that," she said. She looked over the lake and tried to make out an island. She could only see clumps of trees! "Are there really islands in the lake?" she asked.

He nodded and said, "There are a few, but if the girls left Susan where they said, I know right where it is. My dad and I explored it before."

Libby shielded her eyes against the sun to try to see the island. "Will Susan be safe there until we get her?"

"Sure. There aren't any wild animals like bears or wildcats. What could happen to her?"

"Nothing, I guess." Libby shivered. If Susan was really safe, then why was she suddenly frightened for her?

FIVE
The island

Libby watched Clay as he dipped the paddle in the
water. Occasionally he paddled on the other side of
the canoe to keep it on course. The sun sparkled on
the water. Once they were away from shore, the only
sounds Libby heard were the dip of the paddle, the
gentle splash of water, and the thud of her heart.
Finally she spotted two small islands and a larger
one. She could almost feel Susan's fear as she waited
for someone to rescue her.

The rocking of the canoe and the smell of the water
made Libby's stomach do flip-flops. A bitter taste
filled her mouth and she thought she was going to be
sick. She swallowed hard and tried to sit very still.
She didn't want to do anything that would make
them tip over.

"I see someone," said Clay.

Libby gripped the seat tighter and looked at the big
island. At first she only saw trees and a beach, but
then she saw someone waving something orange. "It's
probably Susan waving her life jacket!" said Libby.

Suddenly she couldn't stand the thought of facing Susan. Could she jump out of the canoe and hide in the water? She shivered at the thought. If she could swim better, she might have done that.

"What made you mad enough at your own sister to let those girls do this to her?" asked Clay.

Libby watched a duck land on the water near the shore. "We're not really sisters, you know."

"I know," he said. "But she says you are."

"Yes. She says that." Libby felt even worse.

"You don't have to tell me if you don't want to," said Clay, keeping the paddling smooth and regular.

"I feel too awful to say," said Libby, her head down. She wasn't referring to her motion-sick stomach.

"That's OK." Clay smiled and Libby felt a little better.

Just then Libby heard Susan's shouts for help. Libby breathed a sigh of relief. She was thankful that Susan wasn't in any danger.

"Someone else is there," said Clay.

"Are you sure?" asked Libby in surprise. "I don't see anyone but Susan."

"I saw someone right at the edge of the trees."

"Are you sure?"

Clay frowned. "I did see someone, Libby. I know I did."

"Then where is he?"

"Hiding in the trees." Clay stopped paddling for a minute.

"Libby!" shouted Susan. "It *is* you!"

"We're coming, Susan!" shouted Libby, as Clay started paddling again. She waved her arm high. "We're coming!" She twisted around to see if there was a sinister figure creeping up on Susan.

"Careful, Libby," said Clay. "You're making the canoe rock."

"Sorry. I was just trying to see if I could see the person you saw."

"There!" cried Clay, motioning with his head.

Libby looked, but still couldn't see anyone but Susan.

"It's a girl," said Clay. "I know it is!"

"Maybe Nedra and Gabby abandoned someone else," said Libby.

"Oh, Libby!" shouted Susan, jumping up and down.

Libby saw the tears on Susan's cheeks and she ducked her head in shame. She was very sorry for what she'd done to Susan! But could she tell her that? It would be really terrible if Susan knew that she had known about the plan to abandon her on the island.

The bottom of the canoe scraped the sandy ground at the water's edge. Susan grabbed the canoe and yanked it until it was safely on the shore. She waded out and reached for Libby. "I knew you'd come," said Susan, sobbing. "I prayed you would and you did! God answered and I'm so glad!"

Libby hugged Susan back. "Put your life jacket on and get in, Susan. Hurry!"

Suddenly Clay jumped from the canoe and ran to the sandy beach. "I see you! Come back here!"

"What's he doing?" asked Susan, looking at Clay in surprise.

"He says he saw someone in the trees," whispered Libby. "That's why we have to get out of here."

Susan shook her head and her red-gold ponytails bobbed above her ears. "There's no one else here, Clay. Only me."

"Let's go, Clay!" cried Libby. "Come on! Get back in the canoe right now!"

"I'm going to look around," he said stubbornly.

Libby sighed heavily. She might as well get out and stand while he looked around. Maybe her stomach would stop pitching if she stood on solid ground for a while. She climbed out of the canoe and she and Susan pulled it all the way onto the sand. Water squished in her sneakers and dripped from her jeans onto the sand.

"He won't find anyone," said Susan, watching Clay walk to the trees. "I should know!" She turned to Libby. "You won't believe what Gabby and Nedra did to me!"

Libby's neck and face burned and she looked quickly away from Susan's wide blue eyes.

"They left me! They said we were going to explore the island, but after I got out of the canoe, they just paddled away!" Susan burst into tears and gripped Libby's arm. "It was so awful, Libby!"

Libby pulled away guiltily. "You're safe now," she said quietly.

Susan brushed away her tears with the back of her hands. "I know. It's just that I was so scared! I couldn't believe those girls would just leave me here. I watched them paddle away and no matter how much I yelled to them to come back, they wouldn't." Susan rubbed her hands down her sweatshirt. "And Libby, they laughed! I could hear them laugh! They thought it was funny to leave me behind!"

Libby wanted to sink down in the sand until it covered every guilty inch of her. Abruptly she turned away from Susan to look for Clay. "Clay!" she shouted. "Will you come on? You were seeing things! Nobody's here but us."

"Wouldn't it have been awful if someone had attacked me?" asked Susan, who shivered until her teeth chattered even though the sun was shining brightly.

Clay finally walked out of the trees. His face was red and wet with sweat. He ran to Libby and Susan. "I did see a girl. I know it!"

"Let's just leave," said Libby.

"But we can't leave anyone stranded here," said Susan with a catch in her voice.

Clay turned to face the trees. He cupped his hands around his mouth and shouted, "We are not leaving until you show yourself, so you might as well come talk to us."

Libby jabbed his arm. "Don't say that!"

He didn't look at her, but kept his eyes glued to the trees. "I mean it! I saw you and I know you're a girl! You come out right now! If you don't, I'll send the police out here when we get back to the park office."

"Cut it out, Clay," snapped Libby.

But Clay didn't look at her. He shouted, "We won't leave until you tell us you're all right, so come out and show yourself!"

After a few minutes a teenage girl stepped into sight.

Libby fell back with a gasp.

Susan threw up her hands. "I can't believe I was standing here feeling scared and lonely when you were here all the time!"

The girl just looked at them.

"Well?" asked Clay. "Are you all right?"

"Yes!" cried the girl. "Now, get out of here and leave me alone!"

Libby caught Clay's arm and tugged. "Come on. She said she's all right. Let's go."

Clay pried Libby's fingers loose and shook his head. "No. I can't leave yet. I don't feel right."

Susan took a step toward the girl. "You can ride back to the park with us if you want. Four of us can ride in the canoe."

"I'm staying here," said the girl. "So, get out of here and leave me alone!"

Libby took a step toward the canoe, then stopped because of the look on Clay's face. Something was wrong, really wrong, and only Clay knew what it was.

SIX
The girl

Libby wanted to grab Clay's arm and force him in the canoe, but she didn't move. She hadn't noticed until now that he'd taken off his life jacket, but still wore his red backpack. Water sloshed up on the beach, grabbing at the canoe. A cloud passed over the bright sun for a moment and then disappeared to let the sun shine again.

"I know who you are," Clay said to the girl. He sounded as if he'd been running a long time and couldn't catch his breath. Libby looked anxiously at him. Was he going to have an asthma attack now and not be able to paddle them back to safety?

The stranger flipped back her long dark hair, then stood with her hands defiantly on her lean hips. She wore faded jeans and a black T-shirt that was too large for her slight frame. "Why can't you just leave me alone?" she said angrily. "Is that asking too much?"

Libby didn't think it was, but she didn't say anything.

Susan moved restlessly.

Clay walked toward the girl and Libby and Susan reluctantly fell into step beside him. Libby thought the girl was going to turn and run back into the trees, but she walked toward them, her sneakers spitting sand out behind her as she walked. Finally they stopped just a couple of feet apart from each other.

"I saw you on TV last night," said Clay, nodding his head as he shook his finger at her. "I know I did! You ran away from a detention home in town and the police are looking for you."

Susan gasped.

Libby bit her lip. She knew how terrible a detention home could be and she wanted to tell the girl to run for her life.

The girl trembled and her dark eyes filled with fear, but she squared her shoulders and looked down at Clay. "So what if I did? I won't go back! Now, get out of here and leave me alone."

"Come on, Clay," said Libby. "We don't want to make her go back to a detention home."

"I won't go back!" cried the girl.

"But you'll starve here," said Clay.

"I won't be here that long!" A muscle twitched in the girl's cheek. "Get away from here and leave me alone."

"No!" cried Clay, shaking his head hard. "You can't stay here! And if you make us leave, then I'll tell the police that you're here."

Libby saw the stubborn look on Clay's face and she knew he meant what he said.

Suddenly the girl leaped at Clay and sent him sprawling to the ground. She grabbed and tugged his life jacket out of his hands. It all happened so fast that Libby didn't know what to do.

"Give me your life jacket!" the girl commanded in a hard voice as she reached for Libby.

"No!" Libby backed away, suddenly frightened.

The girl twisted Susan's arm up behind her back, causing her to cry out in pain. "Give me the life jacket or I'll break her arm," she threatened to Libby.

Clay jumped up to help Susan, but the girl kicked his legs from under him and he fell to the ground. He wheezed, fighting for his breath.

Libby nervously unhooked her life jacket and handed it to the girl.

Clay gasped for breath and tried to slip his red backpack off. Libby dropped to the ground and pulled the pack off his back and pushed it into his arms. She glanced up to see the girl run to the canoe with the life jackets. She tossed them into the canoe and pushed the canoe into the water.

"Don't!" cried Libby and Susan together.

Clay frantically searched his backpack for his inhaler. When he finally found it, he used it and hoped that he would be able to breathe easier soon.

Libby watched the canoe with the life jackets drift away from the shore. The girl slowly walked back to them, her fists clenched at her sides and her face set determinedly.

"What are we going to do now?" whispered Susan, looking at Libby.

"I don't know," Libby said.

Clay pounded the sand with his fists and groaned. "I get so frustrated when I can't breathe because then I can't do anything!"

"Are you all right now?" asked Susan with concern.

"I will be in a minute," he said gruffly.

Libby looked at Susan and Clay and suddenly came up with a brilliant idea. She knew a way she could get Chuck to love her again! She could save Susan and Clay from this runaway girl! She could get Susan home safely to her family.

Libby bit her lip and frowned. But how was she going to do it? There was no way off the island except by boat or by swimming. The canoe had floated too far from the island and she was too weak of a swimmer to swim to shore.

"Why did you push our canoe away?" Susan tearfully asked the girl.

She glared at Susan. "I will not go back to that detention home! When I'm gone you can all get out of here and go home again."

"Then you aren't going to hurt us?" asked Clay in surprise. "They said on TV that you're dangerous."

The girl scowled at him. "I'll do what I have to do to stay free."

"Just let me swim after the canoe," said Clay.

Libby could tell he was still too weak to do it. "Don't try it, Clay. It's too far away."

"I could try to get it," said Susan. "I'm a good swimmer."

"No!" cried the girl. "You stay right here!" She grabbed Susan to stop her from swimming after the canoe.

Libby eyed the girl, trying to decide the best way to attack her so Susan would be free. But even though Libby was tall, the girl was taller and probably stronger. Susan wouldn't be any help and Clay was still too weak.

Libby's shoulders sagged as she sighed. Somehow she had to rescue Susan so Chuck would love her again. But if he ever learned that she knew about the plan to abandon Susan, he'd probably want to send her away forever. If she saved Susan, he would keep her, especially if Susan told him how Libby had risked her life just to save her.

Silently Libby started to pray for help, but a terrible black cloud seemed to envelop her. How could she ask Jesus to help her when she'd been so bad?

She turned away from the others as a great sadness welled up inside of her and stopped her from praying.

SEVEN

A rescue team

Libby watched Clay from the corner of her eye. She could see that he was planning to do something. She frowned. Clay was too weak to attack the girl by himself. And he couldn't do anything as long as the girl was holding on to Susan.

"I can't remember your name," said Clay. "I heard it on TV, but I can't remember it."

The girl studied Clay for a minute, then shrugged. "I guess it doesn't matter if you know. My name is Dorothy Pippin, but everybody calls me Pip."

Suddenly Susan tugged free and burst into tears. "I want to go home," she sobbed.

"It's not my fault those girls dumped you here," snapped Pip. "I sure didn't want them to leave you here!"

Libby flushed with guilt. She didn't look at Clay, but she could feel his eyes on her.

Susan rocked back and forth in the sand. "Why would they do such a terrible thing to me? What did I ever do to them?"

"Kids are always doing rotten things to me," said Clay.

"And to me," said Libby savagely.

Pip slapped Susan's shoulder. "Stop crying. It doesn't help at all. I should know."

Just then Libby spotted a canoe heading toward the island. Maybe now they'd be rescued! Jamie Smith had probably reported Susan missing. Or maybe this was just a group of people canoeing for fun.

"Oh, no!" cried Pip as she spotted the canoe. She grabbed Susan and hauled her to her feet.

"You're hurting me!" said Susan with a sob.

"Be quiet or I'll hurt you more," snapped Pip. She twisted Susan's arm up behind her back as she glared at Libby and Clay. "Get in the trees without a sound or I will break her arm. I mean it!"

Libby's heart sank as she walked with the others into the shelter of trees. Would the people in the canoe land on the island and explore it?

Pip stopped them behind a clump of thick bushes. "We'll wait here and see who it is and what they want."

"Maybe it's the person coming after you," said Clay.

Pip scowled at him. "And maybe it's someone after the three of you."

Libby locked her trembling hands together and waited. Clay was breathing easily again. Susan tried to stop crying, but the tears kept rolling down her cheeks.

Several minutes later, the canoe came close enough to the island that Libby could see Mr. Lafferty, one of the parents, and Mr. Everson, one of the teachers. Libby's heart leaped. They were coming to rescue them!

"Don't make a sound!" whispered Pip.

Libby saw the pain on Susan's face and she bit back the cry for help that she'd planned to shout.

The men sat in the canoe just offshore. Libby could easily hear their voices.

"If Libby and Clay were stranded on the island, they'd be out here where we could see them," said Mr. Lafferty.

"You're probably right," said Mr. Everson. "Finding a canoe containing only life jackets isn't a good sign. Hopefully they swam back to the park."

"I'm going to shout for them just in case," said Mr. Lafferty. "Libby! Clay!" He waited, then shouted several more times.

Libby clenched her jaw tight. She wanted to shout to the men, but she knew she didn't dare. She glanced at Clay beside her and knew he felt the same way. She closed her eyes tight and forced back a groan of agony. Oh, she'd caused a lot of trouble just because of her stupid jealousy!

Again Mr. Lafferty shouted, "Libby! Clay! Can you hear me? We came to take you back!"

Libby suddenly realized they weren't calling Susan at all. Didn't they realize that she was missing? She peeked at Susan and saw the puzzled look on her face. Libby's face burned with shame and guilt. Susan was going to ask questions just as soon as Pip let her talk.

"They aren't here," said Mr. Everson. "Let's take a look on shore over there. Maybe there's someone in those cabins who might've seen them."

"I sure hope they're safe," said Mr. Lafferty as he dipped his paddle in the water.

The canoe shot through the water toward the mainland. When they were out of earshot, Pip set Susan free.

"Now we'll just wait it out," Pip said tiredly. "But you kids stay out of sight just in case someone's looking over here with binoculars."

Susan tugged her sweatshirt down over her jeans as she looked questioningly at Libby. "I don't understand why they didn't call my name," she said in a small voice.

Libby's heart jerked. "That *is* funny."

"Very," said Clay, his voice heavy with sarcasm.

"I'm the one missing," said Susan. "You two came after me." She brushed a fly off her arm. "Right, Libby?"

Libby nodded.

"So, how did you know where to find me?" asked Susan. Her blue eyes narrowed as she studied Libby. "Did Nedra or Gabby tell you?"

Libby threw up her hands. "Susan, it's not worth talking about! We have more important things to think about right now. We have to get to shore before the school bus leaves."

"You won't get away that soon," said Pip as she hooked her long hair behind her ears. "You can't leave here until after dark tonight."

"What?" cried Libby, Clay, and Susan, all in one alarmed voice.

"You heard me," said Pip.

Clay shook his head. "Our families will be frightened and worried, Pip."

"I can't help that," she said.

Libby knew Chuck would start searching for them the minute he got the news that they were missing.

"My dad will find me," said Susan with great confidence. "Won't he, Libby?"

She nodded, then had a terrible thought: if *she* was the only one missing, would Chuck look for her? She knew he would. He always helps people in trouble.

"I know a special place in the woods where we'll all hide," said Pip. "So don't go thinking somebody will come here and rescue all of you before I want you to leave."

Libby could see that Clay and Susan felt as frustrated and discouraged as she did.

Susan sank to the ground and sat with her back against a tree. "I still don't understand why Mr. Everson wasn't looking for me. I just don't understand."

"Maybe Jamie didn't tell them you were missing," said Libby as she picked a leaf off a tree branch and studied it.

"Then how did *you* know I was missing?" asked Susan.

Clay opened his pack and pulled out a bag. "Anybody hungry? We could eat what we brought."

Libby shot Clay a look of gratitude.

Pip peeked in the pack. "Do you have an apple?"

"Sure," said Libby as she grabbed her lunch bag from Clay. Susan's questions made her feel awful. She held the apple out to Pip, who bit into it with a sharp snap. Juice squirted out and hit Libby's hand.

"Jamie has my lunch," said Susan.

"You can share ours," said Libby. "Want my sandwich?"

"I have some carrot sticks," said Clay. "And some granola bars."

Libby breathed a sigh of relief as Susan accepted food and ate with them. Maybe Susan wouldn't think to ask again how they'd known where to find her.

Libby bit into her sandwich, but the guilt inside of her made her food taste like cardboard. She tried to forget her guilty feelings as she forced herself to chew and swallow the sandwich.

EIGHT
The fight

With her back against a tree, Libby watched a
squirrel leap from branch to branch, then disappear
from view.

"Libby, I'm not stupid, you know," said Susan as she
refused another carrot stick from Clay. "I know you're
keeping a secret from me. You might as well tell me
what it is."

Libby groaned.

Pip glanced at her watch. "Time's going too slow."

Clay pulled out his video game and started playing.
The beeps echoed in Libby's head.

"Tell me, Libby," said Susan sternly.

"Oh, all right!" Libby pulled her knees to her chin
and hugged her legs tightly. "I found out that Nedra
and Gabby planned to leave you here and so I asked
Clay to help me get you."

Susan was quiet for a while as she studied Libby.
"How did you find out?"

Libby felt her neck and ears burn and she knew
Susan saw the guilty flush.

"Tell me, Libby!" cried Susan.

"Keep your voice down," snapped Pip. "We don't want anyone who might be around here to hear us."

Libby heard the beeping of Clay's game and the painful thud of her heart. "I overheard them planning it," she said in a low, tight voice.

Little by little Susan pulled all the information out of Libby. Susan's face grew redder and redder. Suddenly she leaped to her feet, rushed at Libby, and sent her sprawling in the dirt.

"How could you do that to me, Libby?" cried Susan as she straddled Libby and looked down into her wide hazel eyes. "How?"

Libby squirmed out from under Susan and pushed her away.

"Stop it, you two!" cried Pip, grabbing at Libby's leg.

But Libby pulled away from Pip as Susan flew at her again.

Then out of the corner of her eye, Libby saw Clay leap at Pip. Libby sidestepped Susan and turned to help Clay overpower Pip. Clay tackled Pip and pinned her shoulders to the ground as Libby grabbed her legs.

"Let me go!" cried Pip, struggling.

Susan dropped down beside Libby and glared at her. "I'm going to tell Mom and Dad what you did, Elizabeth Gail Dobbs! And I mean it!"

"This is not the time to have a family quarrel," said Clay breathlessly. "Now that we've got Pip, we have to figure out a way to get off this island."

"Go ahead and leave," snapped Pip.

"We can swim to shore," said Susan.

Libby shivered. "I can't."

64

Susan glared at Libby. "Then stay here with Pip. See if I care!"

Libby hung her head in shame. She deserved every bit of Susan's anger.

"Susan, I have a short rope in my pack," said Clay. "Get it so we can tie Pip up."

"No!" cried Pip. "Don't tie me up!"

"We have to," said Clay. "We can't hold you down forever."

Susan rummaged through the pack and found a short nylon rope. She held it out to Clay, who ordered Pip to sit up. He tied her hands behind her back and buckled his belt around her ankles.

"Now," said Clay. "You will not keep us here any longer. And when we get back I'll tell the police all about you!"

Libby bit her lip and shook her head.

Suddenly Pip burst into heavy sobs.

Susan wrung her hands helplessly. "I feel so bad for her," she whispered.

"So do I," said Libby. "Clay, please don't tell the police. Please don't! Give Pip a chance, will you?"

"She wasn't giving us a chance," said Clay.

"She didn't hurt me while I was here all alone," said Susan. "And she could have."

"That's right," said Libby.

"I can't go back," said Pip with another ragged sob.

"Let's take a vote," said Susan.

Clay rolled his eyes. "How can you girls want to help her after what she did to us?"

"Because she needs help!" cried Susan.

"And do you help everybody that needs help?" asked Clay, sniffing.

"Yes," said Susan.

"She does," said Libby, nodding. "That's the way the whole Johnson family is. I've never met people like them before."

"What makes them so different?" asked Clay.

"God does," said Susan. "Jesus says to love and help others, so we do." She looked at Libby and flushed. "Libby, I'm sorry for getting mad at you."

"I can't believe what I'm hearing," said Clay.

"I am sorry, Libby," said Susan again.

"That's OK," said Libby. "I should've stopped Nedra and Gabby."

"You should've," said Susan. "Why didn't you?"

Libby looked away, her skin hot with shame. "I was . . . was jealous of you."

"Of me? But why?"

"I . . . I don't want to say," whispered Libby.

Susan was quiet for a long time. "I will forgive you no matter what, so you don't have to tell me if you can't."

Tears welled up in Libby's eyes and she blinked them quickly away.

"And I'm sorry for knocking you down," said Susan.

"Me, too," said Libby. It was so easy for Susan to apologize, but Libby often felt the words stick in her throat.

"Now that that's settled we'd better decide what to do with Pip," said Clay dryly.

"I say we set her free," said Libby.

"So do I," said Susan.

"Thank you!" whispered Pip.

"I say we should hear her story first," said Clay. "I think it's only fair. And then we should decide."

"I could lie to you," said Pip stiffly.

"But you won't, will you?" asked Susan softly.

Pip shook her head. "No. I'll tell you the truth."

"Let's untie her first," said Libby.

Clay glanced at his watch. "It's almost one o'clock and the bus leaves the park at two. I don't know if we have time to listen."

"We'll take the time," said Libby as she unbuckled Clay's belt from around Pip's ankles.

Slowly Clay untied Pip's wrists. She rubbed them and moaned with relief.

"Thanks, Clay," said Libby.

"I just hope I did the right thing," he said gruffly.

"You did," said Libby.

"I think so, too," said Susan, smiling at Clay.

Finally he smiled and shrugged. "Let's hear your story, Pip. But make it quick."

Pip pulled her knees to her chin. A faraway look covered her face.

Libby sat beside Susan and leaned eagerly toward Pip.

NINE
Pip's story

*I knew for a long time that Dad didn't like to have me
around, but I was thirteen before I'd admit it to
myself. Mom said I was imagining it when I told her,
but I could tell by her face that she knew it was the
truth. Sometimes I thought he was just under a lot
of pressure at work. I know he hated his job. He
worked at a plastic factory making small parts for
car interiors. I heard him tell Mom that he'd planned
to work there only a few years until he had enough
saved to start his own lawn business. He liked work-
ing outside with flowers and grass. When my brother
Rusty was born, Mom started a savings account for
his college tuition, and then did the same for me when
I was born. Mom's name was on both of our accounts,
but Dad's name wasn't on either of them. It made Dad
mad to have to put that money away every week, but
Mom said they had to.*

   *A few years ago, they had a big fight about that
money. Dad said he needed the money, but Mom
wouldn't let him have it.*

Mom said the money belonged to us kids for our college education. Dad got even angrier and yelled that Mom always put us kids first. It was awful.

Dad said he had a chance to buy Ted Lavery's lawn business. He said Ted had given him first chance on it and he'd told him he'd be over with a check. He asked Mom to go to the bank and get the money. Dad's name wasn't on the accounts so he couldn't just take out the money himself.

I covered my ears with my hands and I was shaking all over at the anger in Dad's voice. But Mom wouldn't give in no matter how angry he got or how loud he shouted. I felt sorry for him, so later I talked to Mom. I told her she could give him the money in my savings account but she said she wouldn't do it.

"Pip, he couldn't make enough money in the lawn business to put you through college. I know how much the Laverys have to struggle to survive. And they have only one child. I will not let your dad have a single penny of your college money," she said.

I knew she meant it. She could be pretty stubborn. I guess I can be too.

After their fight, Dad worked even harder and when he was home, he didn't speak to us or do anything with the family. I felt like it was my fault. I talked to Rusty about it and he said it wasn't my fault at all.

When Rusty started college he was thankful for the money. He still had to get a part-time job to pay his way, but he graduated last month with a degree in business management. Dad wouldn't go to his graduation, but I did. Mom died before he graduated.

It's really hard for me to talk about Mom. She always watched out for us and spent time with us.

Just after Christmas she was driving on an icy road. She lost control, hit a tree, and was killed. I still miss her a lot.

Dad took it hard. I guess he loved Mom a lot, but I'd thought he'd hated her as much as he hated us. He walked around in a daze for a long time. He went to work every day, but wouldn't come home until late every night. I'd try to wait up for him, but I couldn't stay awake most of the time.

Finally about a month ago, he came home right after work and he walked right into my bedroom. He looked excited about something.

"Pip, I need you to take your college money out of the bank and give it to me," he said.

I really wanted to, but I'd already promised it to Rusty so he could go into business for himself right after graduation. He told me that he'd make enough to pay my way through college without any problem. I believed him because he'd never lied to me before. Besides, I really don't plan on going to college. I want to take secretarial training and some computer classes and find a job as a secretary. Rusty and I had already made arrangements to take the money out of the bank the following week.

When I told Dad I couldn't give him the money, his eyes blazed with anger and he slapped me hard across the face. I fell against the bed and just stared at him. I knew my face was bruised. He hauled me up and held my wrist so tight I thought the bones would crack. "I need that money," he said.

"You can't have it!" I shouted. "I don't care if you beat me to death!"

He swore and pushed me down. I fell on the floor,

but I wasn't as hurt by the fall as I was hurt by the way Dad was acting.

He yelled that he was the one who had worked for the money, so it was his and he was going to get it one way or another. Then he stormed out of the house and didn't come back for two days.

I called Rusty and told him what happened. He felt really bad and said I could stay with him until Dad cooled down. So, I packed a bag and went to his apartment. It felt good to be away from the tension and anger in our house. I went to school and caught up on my rest. It seemed like it was hard to rest at home even when I slept. I could sense Dad's anger and I was always worrying about when he'd explode.

One day, after I'd been at Rusty's for almost three weeks, a woman stopped me on my way home from school. She said she was from child welfare and that I had to go with her. She said my dad had said I ran away from home and he insisted I return there.

I told her I was living with my brother now, but she just said I couldn't stay with him without permission from my legal guardian—my dad.

She took me home and explained the law that says I have to live there. She wouldn't listen when I told her about Dad. When she left I went right back to Rusty's. Dad reported me again and the child welfare worker came and got me. I told Dad that I was going to live with Rusty no matter what he said. He didn't say anything to me, but he had the police put me in a detention home for a night.

I was taken to court and the judge said I had to stay with my father, not my brother. I tried to tell the judge about Dad, but he wouldn't listen to me. Dad had already told him lies about me. He said that I stayed out all night with my boyfriend. I didn't even have a boyfriend, but the judge wouldn't listen. Dad also said that he knew I was doing drugs, but I never had.

When we got home Dad said if I'd give him the money he'd let me go live with Rusty. By then I'd already given it to Rusty and he'd already used most of it. "I don't have the money," I said.

"What? Do you expect me to believe that lie?" he yelled.

I sat huddled on a kitchen chair, scared of what he'd do to me and to Rusty if he knew I'd given him the money.

"Get your savings account book and let's go to the bank right now," Dad said, sounding calmer. "I promise I'll pay back every dime, Pip. Is that what you want to hear?"

"Dad, I don't have the money." I could hardly breathe. "I can show you my book and you'll see I'm telling the truth."

"Show me the book!" he snapped.

I ran to my bedroom while he stayed in the kitchen. I didn't know what he'd do to me when he found that the money really was gone. I grabbed some of my things, climbed out my window and ran as fast as I could. I stopped at a pay phone and called Rusty. He picked me up right away. I told him what had happened and he said he'd talk to Dad.

"I don't want Dad to hurt you, Rusty," I said, sobbing. "If he knows I gave you the money he'll do something terrible. I just know it! Please promise you won't tell him. Please!"

"All right," Rusty said. "But I don't like it."

The next day the police arrested me. This time Dad told the judge that I'd stolen money from him and wouldn't follow the rules of the house.

"I want her put away where she can get some help," Dad said, sounding very sincere. I wanted to scream at him. Dad sounded really sad when he said, "I can't do a thing with her. I have had a hard time with her since her mother died. She needs help."

I turned to the judge and said, "My brother will let me live with him. He's twenty-one and has a business of his own. Please, let me go live with him!"

"No!" shouted Dad. "He's a bad influence on her. I won't agree to that!"

Then I knew that Dad really and truly hated me. He was having me locked away because I wouldn't sign my money over to him. I tried to tell the judge, but he wouldn't listen to me. He said I did need help in a detention home. They said Rusty couldn't visit me or have any contact with me. But Rusty sent his girlfriend to tell me that he had done everything he could to get custody of me, but the judge would not allow it.

I only had to stay in the home until I was eighteen, so I tried to tell myself that three years would pass quickly. But it was hard in the home. Two girls, Mickey and Gina, started picking on me the day I arrived. They were both fifteen, too, and had been in a street gang. Gina said they'd knifed an old man for his money, but they hadn't been caught for that. They were put in detention for possession of drugs, for skipping school, and for running away from home. They took my food and my clothes and when they started a fight, they said it was my fault.

It was awful! I was there for over two weeks and it felt like twenty years!

I became friends with a girl named Cindy Nash. Her mom had put her in the home because she'd gotten remarried and didn't want Cindy around. Cindy was pretty and smart and I liked her a lot.

One day, we were sitting together on the sofa in the day room when Micky and Gina ran in. They looked guilty about something, but I wasn't about to start a conversation with them.

Gina plopped down next to me. She was overweight, had dirty brown hair, and smelled like she hadn't taken a shower for a week. "So, Pip, did you get your math done for tomorrow?"

"Yes," I said. I couldn't imagine why she'd even care.

"That's good," said Gina. "Hey, Mickey, she got it done."

"Great," said Mickey.

"So, Pip, I need your paper," said Gina.

"No way!" I cried. I started to jump up, but Gina caught my hand and bent back my thumb until it brought tears to my eyes.

"Give me your math paper, Pip," said Gina.

"Leave her alone," whispered Cindy.

"Stay out of this," snapped Mickey, kicking Cindy in the ankle. "We need that math paper now, Pip."

"You think you got the answers right?" asked Gina. "We don't want to copy no paper that has wrong answers."

I knew they were all right. I was good in math. I should've been in algebra, but it conflicted with my bookkeeping class. "They're right," I said. I didn't want a broken thumb over a dumb math paper. "It's under the coffee table."

Mickey picked up my book and lifted out my paper. She was slim and pretty with green eyes and blonde hair pulled back in a ponytail. "This is it, Gina."

Gina gave my thumb one last painful squeeze and let me go. She pushed herself up and stood beside Mickey. "We'll get this copied right away and then old Karen will let us watch TV."

They ran to their room and I sighed in relief. I felt Cindy trembling beside me. I looked at her and saw tears running down her cheeks.

"What's wrong, Cindy?" I asked in alarm.

"I don't want to stay here," she said with a sob. "I want to be home in my own room so I don't have to be around people like those two."

"I know," I said. We usually got treated all right in the detention home, but we felt like prisoners. We had no choice but to stay there, plus we had to share the home with eight other girls, most of them like Gina and Mickey. Some of them worse. I knew Cindy had been beaten up twice since I'd arrived. Mickey had wanted a bottle of her perfume and a pair of yellow pajamas that Cindy's mom had sent to her. Cindy wouldn't give them to Mickey when she'd asked for them so Mickey had beat her up to get them. Mickey went around bragging to everyone that Cindy had given her the gifts just because she wanted to. I'm sure no one believed her, but they didn't say anything.

As far as I knew, all the others belonged in the home, but I knew Cindy and I didn't. We'd both tried to tell Karen Ducey, the woman in charge of the home. Karen was all right, but she didn't believe us when we said we were put in there because our parents had lied. I knew nobody would ever believe us and help get us out of the home. I couldn't stand to think of spending the next three years there. Even two weeks in that place made me crazy.

"Pip," whispered Cindy. "I'm going to run away."

"Oh, Cindy!"

"I've been thinking about it since Mom put me in here last month. I can't stand it any longer."

"But where will you go?" I asked. I knew she didn't have any family.

"I don't know, but I have to get out of here." Tears welled up in her blue eyes. "Yesterday I hit Stacey!"

Stacey was fourteen years old and a little mentally slow. She was always bothering Cindy. She'd sneak in Cindy's room and try on her clothes and use her makeup.

"I never hit anyone in my life!" Cindy said. "But I hit Stacey because she tore my favorite blouse. I actually hit her! If I stay here I might start beating up people like Mickey does."

"But you can't live on the streets," I said. I'd read about and heard about what happened to girls on the streets. I know she had heard the same stories.

"I'll decide what to do once I'm out of here," she said. I could tell by the stubborn look on her face that she was serious.

"I'll try to talk to Rusty," I said. "Maybe he'll let you stay with us. Or maybe with his girlfriend, Rilla. She's nice. She has her own apartment. Maybe she'd let you share it if you helped with the bills and everything."

"Oh, Pip! I can get a job! I'll be sixteen soon, so I can drop out of school, maybe go to night classes later."

So when Rilla came to visit the next day I told her
all about Cindy. We talked outdoors away from the
home so nobody could overhear us. I didn't want to
spoil Cindy's chances.

"I'll see what I can do," Rilla said.

"Thank you!" I hugged her hard and she hugged
me. It felt so good! Mom had always hugged me, but
lately I hadn't gotten as many hugs as I needed.

"Now, tell me how you are," Rilla said.

So I told her about the math paper and all the other
things that happened and she got mad. She thought
it was terrible that Dad had sent me there and she
said she would try to get me out.

"Rilla," I said as I took her hand. "Tell Rusty that
I've been thinking about running away. I wouldn't
go right to his place because that's where they'd look
for me."

"Where would you go?" asked Rilla.

"To Pontiac State Park," I said. I told her all about
this island and how Rusty and I had explored it lots
of times. I said I'd swim out. I'd done it before with
Rusty and I knew if I paced myself, I could do it
alone. I could stay on the island for the weekend,
then Rusty could come for me. Suddenly I knew I
wasn't just thinking about running away, but I had
decided that I was going to do it no matter what.
"When I get to Rusty's I'll cut my hair and dye it red
and I'll buy a pair of glasses to wear. I'll change
my name and everything. I can stay lost until I'm
eighteen if I really try, Rilla!"

"Oh, Pip! I'm so sorry it's come to this," she said.

"Me too," I said.

So Cindy and I decided that we'd sneak out of

school early on Friday. That was just last Friday. She'd go to Rilla's because the authorities wouldn't even think about looking there, and I'd come to this island. Rusty is supposed to come get me tonight. I don't know if Cindy is OK or not. I hope she is!

If I get sent back to the detention home, I'll probably be under closer watch or else sent to a different home so that I'll never be able to get to Rusty.

He's coming tonight and I'm going with him. I will not go back to that home! I won't! I'll live with Rusty until I can be on my own.

I've come too far to let anything or anyone stop me. I'm desperate and I'm scared. And I want my brother!

TEN
The storm

After Pip's story, Libby brushed stinging tears from
her eyes, then glanced at Clay and saw that he was
doing the same thing. Susan walked right up to Pip
and put her arms around her and held her tight, just
like Vera would've done.

"We won't turn you in," said Susan, her voice
muffled against Pip. "My dad will help you!"

Pip held on to Susan tightly, tears streaming down
her face.

Libby nodded, but she couldn't speak around the
lump in her throat. She'd been around a lot of girls
just like Mickey and Gina. In fact, before she'd
accepted Jesus into her life, she'd been as bad as
Mickey and Gina. It had been easier to get along with
rough kids if she was rough also.

"I won't turn you in," said Clay as he jumped up and
slipped on his backpack. "But we have to get out of
here right away before more people come to look for us."

"You three go ahead," said Pip, smiling for the first
time since they'd met her. "I can stay hidden without

any problem. And thanks! For everything!" She smiled wider at Susan.

Susan shook her head. "You don't have to stay here, Pip. We'll take you right to my dad and he'll take care of you."

"But she'd have to ride the bus and people would see her," said Clay.

"Oh, that's right," said Susan.

"We'll call Dad when we get to school," said Libby. She glanced out at the lake and shivered, suddenly remembering. "Clay, I can't swim all the way to shore."

"She can't," said Susan. "It is a long way. I don't know if I can either."

Clay sighed heavily.

"I'm really sorry I pushed your canoe away," said Pip.

"Hey, I know what we can do!" cried Clay with a delighted laugh.

"What?" asked Libby. She'd come to realize that Clay had some pretty good ideas.

"We'll find a log and we can all hang on to it and swim to shore. It'll work." Clay puffed out his chest and looked very pleased with himself. "I can even tie my rope around it and we can hang on to the rope. That would make it easier."

"Are you sure it'll work?" asked Libby.

"It will," said Pip before Clay could answer. "Rusty and I did it one time."

"I'm willing to try it," said Susan, who usually was afraid to try new things.

Libby hugged her thin arms against her chest. A blue jay shrieked from a tall pine. A chipmunk ran

82

into sight and dodged under a bush. Finally Libby nodded. "I guess I'll try it, too."

"Good for you, Libby," said Susan, smiling.

"We'd better hurry and find a log," said Clay. He looked at his watch. "We'll miss the school bus, but we can get to a phone and call our families."

"I know where to look for a log," said Pip. "Years ago someone cut down some trees deeper into the woods. You should be able to find a log that'll work for you. Follow me." Pip turned and ran into the woods, leaves and twigs crackling under her feet.

Clay ran after her, and Susan and Libby followed. Twigs caught at Libby's hair, tugging it hard enough to make her cry in pain. Her foot caught in a trailing vine. She pitched forward, but caught herself before she fell.

Pip stopped in the area she had mentioned and said, "Look around here. I'm sure we can find a log that you can use."

Finally Clay found a log that he said would work. It was about eight feet long and about one foot around.

"Can we carry it?" asked Susan as she nudged it with the toe of her sneaker.

"It's an old log so it's not very heavy," said Clay. He started sniffing again. The mold and decay made it hard for him to breathe.

Libby looked around and suddenly realized how dark it was in the woods. "I didn't think it would be so dark in here," she said.

Pip glanced up in alarm. "It's not usually." She looked up at the sky, barely visible through the branches, and frowned. "Look at the sky! And it suddenly feels colder!"

"A storm's coming!" cried Clay. "Let's get this log to the water and get out of here!"

Frantically Libby ran to Clay to help carry the log. At Clay's shout they hoisted the log and carried it back the way they'd come. The bark bit into Libby's arms and hands. The weight tugged on her arms and hurt her shoulder and back. She bit her lip to keep from begging him to stop to rest. Suddenly the wind began to blow, whipping the tops of the trees back and forth.

"Put the log down!" shouted Clay above the noise of the wind as they reached the edge of the woods.

Libby lowered the log to the ground in unison with the others. She rubbed the scraped places on her arms and looked at the marks left by the bark. She trembled at the sound of the wind. Choppy waves rushed up on the beach.

"A storm's coming fast," said Pip.

"We can't swim in that water!" cried Susan, pointing just as the waves got higher.

"We're stuck here until the storm passes," said Clay, sounding defeated.

"What about Rusty?" asked Pip close to tears. "He can't get out here to get me!"

Susan patted Pip's arm.

Suddenly thunder cracked and lightning zigzagged across the ever-darkening sky.

Libby looked frantically around for shelter.

"It's going to rain," said Pip. "Follow me and I'll take you to my hideout."

"We can't be under a tree when lightning is flashing," said Clay.

"We'll be safe in my shelter," said Pip. "Come on!"

They ran back the way they'd come. Libby noticed how the wind blocked out the noise of running feet— but not the sound of blood pounding in her ears.

Just as Libby reached the shelter, rain pelted from the sky. Pip dropped to her knees and crawled under a low-hanging pine bough. Susan, Clay, and Libby followed. It was dark inside, but they were still able to see. The scent of pine was overpowering. Libby sat on the ground covered with pine needles as she looked around at Pip's hiding place. She had a supply of food and even a sleeping bag.

"Rusty and I brought some things out and left them here a few weeks ago," Pip said. "We used to come here on Sunday afternoons just to get away from Dad's anger." She took a deep, steadying breath. "I brought a few things to eat when I came Friday."

"It's not bad at all in here," said Susan.

Thunder boomed. Libby jumped and Susan shrieked.

"I hate storms," said Pip, shivering.

Clay hugged his pack. "I'm not my best in storms," he whispered hoarsely. "I don't want lightning to fry me to a crisp."

"I don't want a big old tree to fall on me," said Pip.

Susan took a deep breath, then said, "If Dad was here with us, he'd tell us that we don't have to be afraid because Jesus is with us and angels are watching over us to keep us safe."

Libby nodded.

Susan took another deep breath and smiled at the others. "The Bible says to think on good things, on whatever is pure and holy. When you think on good things it keeps your mind off bad things."

"That's true," said Pip.

"The Bible also says to guard your heart. That means to push away all those terrible thoughts, like being fried to a crisp or smashed under a tree, and think about what God has provided for us. He did give us angels to watch out for us. If we could see them we'd probably see them holding up the trees around us so we don't get smashed. And he's holding back the lightning from striking us." Susan smiled. "I'd rather think about angels than about scary things."

"Me, too," said Libby. She was proud of Susan for speaking up.

"I didn't know about angels watching over us," said Clay. "I'm glad I know that now."

Libby listened to the others talk, but she didn't say anything. She knew it was her fault that they were all here right now instead of on the bus riding back to school. She'd spent so much time being jealous and trying to get even with Susan that she'd let her imagination go wild. She'd spent so much time thinking that Chuck didn't love her that she forgot to think about how much Jesus loved her.

"Thank you, Jesus, for your love," she silently prayed. "I'm sorry for being jealous and for being mean to Susan. Please forgive me." Libby knew that Jesus was always willing and ready to forgive her when she came to him. All of a sudden the darkness that covered her heart lifted. Light seemed to explode inside her. Jesus was her Friend and her Savior! He had forgiven her and he loved her just as he always had. He had never stopped loving her, even when she felt that he did.

Libby smiled and slid a little closer to Susan.

ELEVEN
The log

Libby woke with a start. She hadn't realized that she'd dozed off. She saw that the others had, too. She listened and realized that the wind and rain had stopped. She peeked out of the shelter. Birds sang in the trees and a squirrel chattered. She caught a flash of red and knew it was a cardinal, then saw a flash of blue and knew it was a blue jay. It cried in outrage and another one answered.

"What time is it?" muttered Libby. Both Clay and Pip had watches, but she didn't.

She crawled to Clay and peered at his watch. It was almost seven o'clock! "Hey! Wake up, you guys! We fell asleep!"

Clay sat up with a start and whistled when he saw what time it was.

"I didn't even know I fell asleep," said Susan with a yawn. She rubbed her eyes.

Pip trembled. She picked pine needles from her long, dark hair. "Now that it's time for you guys to leave, I don't want you to go."

"What?" said Clay gruffly. "You're not going to change your mind and keep us prisoners again, are you?"

"She wouldn't do that," said Susan.

Pip shook her head. "I was thinking maybe I'd better go with you. Rusty could get in a lot of trouble if he came for me and the police caught him."

"The police will be out looking for the three of us," said Libby. "And you don't want them to see you, Pip."

"That's right," said Clay. "I think you should come with us right now and we'll watch for anyone looking for us."

"Dad will help you, Pip," said Susan. "You can go home with us and call Rusty from there."

Pip shook her head. "I won't go to your home, but I will swim off the island with you and call Rusty as soon as we find a phone."

"Let's go then," said Clay.

Pip led the way back to where they'd left the log. Libby's neck hurt from sleeping on the ground. She twisted her head and tried to relieve the pain. Cool wind ruffled her tangled hair.

"Let's carry the log to the edge of the water," said Clay.

Libby ran to her assigned spot and lifted the log when Clay said to. The log felt heavier than it had before. The wet bark rubbed against her arms. Her feet sank into the wet sand.

At the edge of the lake, Clay tied his rope loosely around the log. "All four of us can hang on to the rope like this," he said, showing them how to slip their arms through the rope. "Or you can put your arm over the log like this. You paddle with your free arm and your legs. It should work. I hope."

"I have a swimsuit on under my jeans," said Pip. "Do you girls? Clay?"

"We do," said Susan and Libby, and Clay nodded. One of the rules for the day was to wear a swimsuit under their clothes. Each year, several kids went swimming or fell in the lake on purpose. To solve the problem of riding home in wet clothes, the teachers had insisted that all students wear swimsuits under their regular clothes. Libby was glad for the rule now.

"I'll get the plastic bag I used when I came," said Pip. "We can stick our clothes and shoes in it and tie it to the log. When we reach the shore, we'll have dry things to wear."

A few minutes later Libby stepped into the water, dressed only in her bright blue swimsuit. She shivered more from fright than the cool wind as she helped ease the log into the warm water. Wearing a black and pink one-piece suit, Pip tied the plastic bag to the log.

"Clay, I have a good idea," said Pip as she waded around the log.

"What is it?" he asked.

"You and I could swim behind the log and push it along," said Pip.

Clay tapped his finger to his lips in thought, then finally nodded. "It should work. Let's try it that way."

Libby swam on the right side of the log and Susan on the left. She knew Susan hated the yellow and green swimsuit she was wearing and had almost left home without it this morning. She was probably glad Vera had made her wear it.

Libby wrinkled her nose at the fishy-smelling water and forced back the sick feeling sloshing around in her stomach. She gripped the rope with her right hand and used her other hand to pull the log at the same time Susan did. She kept her legs straight back and kicked her feet and the log moved slowly toward the shore. Libby wished they'd shoot across the water the way they had in the canoe.

After a while she noticed that they'd changed directions. She heard Clay shout to Pip that he'd kick alone for a while to turn back in the right way. Finally the log turned, and both Clay and Pip kicked again.

Libby's legs ached and she wanted to quit kicking, but she knew she couldn't. Her left arm felt too heavy to hold up as she sliced through the water with it. The rope cut into her right hand, hurting it more than when Goosy Poosy had pecked her. How she'd love to sink down on her comfortable bed safe at home!

"Rest time!" Clay finally shouted.

Panting for breath, Libby flung both arms over the log just as Susan did. Clay and Pip both turned on their backs and floated along beside the log. The sun sank lower and lower and soon hid behind a grove of trees. Libby was so tired that she didn't want to move ever again. She knew Susan was tired too, because she was very quiet and she usually talked more than anyone else in the family. Libby often had a hard time pushing words out of her mouth, but Susan never did. Sometimes Libby wished she could be more like Susan. But Susan couldn't play the piano.

Libby smiled again. She had a special gift for piano.

Vera often said that she was learning piano quicker than she'd ever expected. Libby had a dream to be a concert pianist and play piano in front of thousands of people. She worked hard to make that dream come true.

She thought of her water-wrinkled hands and wondered if she and her water-wrinkled hands would ever make it back home again!

She frowned and shook her head. She would not think such a terrible thought! She remembered what Susan had said about putting down her vain imaginings and thinking on good things. She would not drown. She would live, and someday she'd sit at a beautiful grand piano before a huge crowd of cheering people and she'd play like no one else before her had played!

"Rest over!" called Clay. "We have to try harder so we make it to land before dark. We won't be able to rest again until we reach land."

Libby groaned as she got in position. Could she make it? Yes! She turned her head to keep from swallowing water and started kicking with her feet and paddling with her left hand. Twice she swallowed water, then choked and coughed. She felt so tired she wanted to let go and just sink down to rest, but she refused to let go. She swam on and on, never stopping, no matter how badly she wanted to.

Suddenly, just as she thought she couldn't swim another inch, a fresh burst of energy leaped through her. It felt so good she wanted to tell the others, but she knew she couldn't talk until they reached shore.

She frowned thoughtfully as she stroked and kicked. What had caused the burst of energy?

Suddenly she knew. Chuck, Vera, Toby, Ben and Kevin would be praying for them, praying for their safety. Libby knew that God answered prayer, and worked miracles. She knew he had just worked a miracle for her. She smiled, making sure her head was turned so no fishy-smelling or fishy-tasting lake water could splash into her mouth or nose.

Now she knew she could make it. "Thank you, heavenly Father," she silently prayed. "Thank you for extra strength for Susan and Pip and Clay. Thank you for helping us reach shore safely!"

After a long time Libby felt her toes scrape bottom. She dropped her legs and stood up with a glad shout. "We made it!" she cried.

Susan burst into tears and sagged down in the shallow water. "We made it! Thank you, Jesus!"

Pip untied the plastic bag and tossed it up on land. She stumbled after it and collapsed beside it, her head on the bag.

Clay dragged himself to shore and dropped to the rough grass at the edge. "We did it," he said weakly.

Libby crawled on shore and flopped on her stomach on the hard ground. She shivered at the sudden chill of the air after being in the warm water. There was no sandy beach here, but only rocks, grass and underbrush. It was almost too dark to see. There was already a star twinkling in the sky.

Frogs croaked and other night sounds joined in. Off in the distance a siren wailed.

Finally Pip opened the plastic bag and everyone dressed again. Clay slipped on his backpack and looked around. "We didn't land where I'd planned, but I think I know where we are."

"I'm so cold!" whispered Susan, her teeth chattering as she pulled her sweatshirt down in place. "Oh, that's better!"

"There should be a cabin nearby," said Pip.

Libby's stomach growled with hunger, but she knew they'd already eaten everything they had. The water from her bright blue swimsuit seeped through her jeans and sweatshirt. Her hair hung in wet tangles down to her thin shoulders. "Which way do we go?" she asked.

"That way," said Clay, pointing to the right.

"That way," said Pip, pointing to the left.

They looked at each other and laughed, but Libby didn't think it was funny at all. She didn't want to spend the night away from home in a strange place.

"That way," said Clay, nodding. "I know it is, Pip."

"And I know it's that way," Pip said as she looped a stretch band around her hair. "I know, Clay!"

"Maybe there are cabins no matter which way we go," said Susan as she leaned over and squeezed water from her long hair.

"That could be," said Clay. "So, who wants to decide which way we go?"

"You!" cried all three girls at once as they pointed to Clay.

He laughed and shrugged. "If that's the way you want it. Follow me," he said, lifting his hand high as if he was leading a march.

Libby grinned as she fell into step.

TWELVE
A house in the woods

Libby suddenly bumped into Clay, who had stopped directly in front of her. "Sorry," she said. It was dark out, but they were still able to see where they were walking. Her mind had been home on the Johnson's farm and she hadn't noticed when he'd stopped.

"Here's the dirt road I knew about," he said, wheezing. He fumbled in his pack and found his inhaler and breathed. Weakly he sank to the ground. "I have to rest a minute."

Susan dropped down beside him. "It feels like we've been walking for hours!"

"It's been only half an hour," said Pip, sinking to the ground beside Susan. "But it seems longer because there isn't a path to follow. I'm all scratched up by those briars we went through."

"Me, too," said Libby, gingerly touching her arm where it burned from a deep scratch. She sat beside Clay, who was trying to breathe normally again. "Is there anything I can do to help you, Clay?" she asked.

"You guys might have to leave me and go on alone for help," he said between gasps for air.

Just then Libby saw the flashing red light on top of a police car. Was it coming their way? She nudged Pip and pointed. "Look!"

Pip leaped up. "I've got to get out of here!"

"We'll go with you," said Susan, springing to her feet. "We can't leave you out here all by yourself."

Pip and Susan crept off the dirt road and Libby started to follow, but stopped when she noticed that Clay wasn't behind her. She turned and whispered, "Come on, Clay."

"I can't get up," he said, wheezing. "I'm too weak."

Libby took his arm and helped him up. "Lean on me," she said sharply. "We must hurry!" She could see the police car was closer and soon would catch them in its headlights.

Clay stumbled and almost dragged them both down, but Libby put her arm around his waist and walked him back among the trees at the side of the road.

"We're here," whispered Pip.

Libby finally spotted the patch of white of Susan's sweatshirt. She eased Clay to the ground beside Susan and sank down beside him.

"They're probably looking for us," said Susan.

"Or for me," said Pip in a low, tight voice. "Maybe Dad remembered all the time Rusty and I spent out here and told the police to check the area."

"Well, they won't find you," snapped Susan. "You're safe with us."

Libby watched the police car lights slowly cut through the darkness on the road a few feet from

96

her. The hum of the engine grew louder and louder. Libby held her breath as it passed the spot where they were hiding. Maybe they should just leap out and save themselves and let Pip fend for herself.

No! The word echoed inside her head and felt louder than if she'd yelled it out loud. It was almost as loud as Clay's wheezing. She knew Susan would not leave Pip, and neither would she!

The taillights of the police car vanished and she knew the car had turned a corner. "Shall we go now?" she asked.

"That road goes all the way around the lake," said Pip. "It would probably be safe to go." But she didn't move.

"Clay?" asked Libby.

"Pip's right," said Clay in a weak voice.

"Susan, help me with Clay," said Libby as she helped Clay stand.

Susan pulled Clay's arm around her shoulders. "I'm ready," she said.

Libby, with Clay and Susan, took a step forward. Suddenly bright lights cut through the night. A red light flashed. The police car was coming back toward them! Sweat popped out on Libby's forehead and prickles of fear stung her nerve endings.

She pulled back and they all ducked down just as the car drove past. "That was close," she said.

"Close," said Pip with a shiver that Libby felt.

"He must have found a place to turn around up there," said Susan. "Maybe in a driveway."

"A cabin?" whispered Libby.

"Let's go look," said Clay. He tried to stand on his own, but sagged back down.

Libby and Susan hoisted him up and cautiously walked back to the dirt road with Pip close at Susan's side. As they walked, crickets played their little fiddles and bullfrogs sang the bass while peepers joined in with the melody.

Libby stumbled on a rut in the road, but caught herself before she fell. She knew if she'd taken a tumble, Susan and Clay would've gone down with her. They finally reached the place where the car had turned around. "It's a driveway," said Libby. "See the mailbox?"

"I can barely make out a house," said Pip. "There aren't any lights on. It's probably someone's week-end home or maybe whoever lives here is gone right now."

"Maybe there's a phone," said Libby. "We should at least check it out. Right, Clay?"

"Right," he said weakly.

"I hope they don't have a dog that bites," said Susan.

"If there was a dog it'd be barking already," said Pip.

They walked as quickly as they could to the house and up on the front porch. Libby and Susan eased Clay to the top step where he sat, fighting for breath.

"You knock, Libby," said Susan, standing back from the door.

"I'll stay out of sight in case someone is here," said Pip, standing behind an evergreen tree.

Libby knocked. The sound seemed to burst out into the night. She waited, then knocked again.

"Nobody's home," said Susan in a discouraged voice.

Frustrated, Libby grabbed the doorknob and rattled it. To her surprise, the knob turned and the door opened. She didn't know what to do. Finally, she gathered all her courage and called, "Anybody home?" She waited, then called two more times.

"I guess nobody's home," whispered Susan.

"We have to see if there's a phone," said Libby. It was so hard to take the first step into the house! But she knew they had to go inside. Clay and Pip needed help, and she and Susan needed to call home for Chuck to come get them.

Libby searched the wall next to the door and finally found a light switch. She clicked it on and lights blazed overhead. Her stomach tightened as she waited for someone to leap out and demand to know what they were doing. But no one leaped out and she stepped all the way inside. The others followed, Pip helping Clay.

Libby looked around and found that they were in a large kitchen. Two doors led off from it, one to a bathroom and another to a bedroom. She smelled a faint aroma of cedar over the closed-in smell. She looked all around for a telephone. She found a jack in the bedroom where the phone should've been.

"There's no phone," she said in great disappointment as she slowly walked back to the others. Clay sat on a kitchen chair and leaned weakly on the table. Pip stood behind him and Susan stood near the refrigerator that was humming quietly.

"I'm thirsty," said Susan. "I don't think it would hurt to get a drink, do you?"

"I don't," said Pip. She found some paper cups, turned on the cold water, and let it run for a while before filling a cup of water for each of them.

The water ran down Libby's dry throat and washed

away the sandpaper feeling. Her stomach growled with hunger, and she knew the others were hungry, too. She opened the refrigerator and looked inside. Several bottles of salad dressing lined the shelf on the door. A bag of apples lay on the top shelf beside a big bottle of catsup. She hesitated, then took out four apples and handed them around. She pulled a dollar bill from her pocket and stuck it inside the bag with the apples.

She bit into the cold, crisp apple, sending juice spraying. Every bite tasted delicious. She ate it until only the stem and a few seeds remained. She noticed the others had done the same. She walked to Clay's side and smiled down at him. "Are you feeling better, Clay?"

He nodded. "I can finally breathe again. It helped just to sit quietly for a while. I won't be able to walk fast, but I might be able to walk by myself now."

Libby licked her dry lips and said, "At our house when something's wrong with somebody in the family, we always pray together for them. We can pray for you right now." She looked helplessly at Susan. Praying for others was still pretty new to Libby, but Susan had been doing it all her life.

"Sure, we'll pray for you," said Susan. "Jesus will help you." Susan caught Pip's hand and pulled her to her side. "We'll all pray for you."

Clay shrugged. "I never had anybody pray for me before."

Libby bowed her head and waited for Susan to pray, but when she nudged her, Libby prayed, "Thank you, heavenly Father, for taking care of all of us and for helping us get safely off the island. We pray now for Clay, that you'll give him supernatural strength so he can walk with us to find a phone. And help us to find a phone soon. Heal Clay of his allergies so he doesn't have to sniff all the time. And help Pip get safely to her brother. In Jesus' name. Amen."

"There!" said Susan brightly. "Jesus answers prayer. So, let's go find a phone!"

Libby couldn't look at Clay. She trembled over her boldness, but she felt as if she was walking on air as she followed the others out the door. She turned off the light and closed the door securely. She waited with the others until their eyes were adjusted to the darkness, then walked off the porch and down the driveway.

Just then a twig snapped and something snorted. Everyone huddled together and stood very still.

"What was that?" whispered Libby.

"Probably just a deer," whispered Clay.

Libby listened, her breath caught in her throat. She heard something run into the trees, then all was quiet except for the crickets, the bullfrogs and the little peepers. "It's gone," she finally said. She lowered her voice. "Let's go."

"We'll go the way the police car went," said Clay, sounding like his old self again.

"Good idea," said Pip.

"Lead the way," said Susan.

"We have a phone call to make," said Libby with a breathless laugh.

THIRTEEN
Decisions

Libby stopped short, her feet tired from walking on the rough dirt road. "We've come a long way. I thought we'd see another house by now."

"I think we're almost to the highway," said Clay.

"Oh, no!" cried Pip. "I think you're right! I can't let anyone see me!"

Just then car lights flashed toward them and Libby, with the others beside her, ran into the safety of the trees. The car passed, driving slow. Soon the taillights disappeared from view. After a long time Libby said, "I think it's safe now."

"This is amazing," said Clay, sniffing.

"What?" asked Libby.

"I can breathe! I mean I can *really* breathe!" Clay breathed deeply to prove his point.

Susan laughed. "I told you Jesus answers prayers," she said.

"He does," said Libby just above a whisper. She was still getting used to praying and having her prayers answered. A branch caught against her jeans as she stepped onto the road. She tugged it free and tossed it aside.

"I sure hope he helps me and Rusty," said Pip as they walked side by side down the dirt road.

"He will," said Susan with great confidence. "I still say you should go home with us tonight and let Dad help you."

"You should," said Libby.

"Well, I don't know," said Pip slowly. "I know he's your dad and you trust him, but I don't know if I can."

Libby knew just how Pip felt. It had taken her a long time to realize she could trust Chuck. Sometimes she still forgot she could.

A bat darted across the moonlit sky and an owl hooted. The smell of the lake was strong in the air.

"Dad is full of love," said Susan.

"My dad loves me," said Clay. "But I don't know if he'd love other people enough to help them. I should ask him when I get home."

"Your dad couldn't love me," said Pip as she flipped her tangled hair over her thin shoulder. "He doesn't even know me."

Susan laughed softly. "Dad is like Jesus. Full of love. He has enough love for everyone. Enough love for you, too, Pip."

Susan's words burst into Libby's heart and she almost gasped aloud. Chuck did love like Jesus! Chuck did have enough love for everyone! For Susan. For the boys. For Vera. Libby's heart raced. For her! Chuck had enough love for both her and Susan!

Tears filled Libby's eyes but she quickly blinked them away. She had been so jealous and so selfish that she'd forgotten that Chuck had more love than anyone she'd ever known. He hadn't stopped loving her! She'd tried to take all of his time so Susan wouldn't have any. She hadn't wanted to share Chuck and she'd taken it out on Susan. Chuck gave her as much time as he did the others in the family, sometimes more time. How could she have thought he didn't love her? How could she have been so mean to Susan? "Forgive me, Jesus," she said under her breath. "I am so sorry!"

As soon as she could, she'd tell Susan everything. She knew Susan would forgive her easily because she was a very forgiving person.

"If you're sure," Libby heard Pip say.

"Dad will want to help you, Pip," said Susan. "Won't he, Libby?"

"He will do everything he can to help you," said Libby passionately. She laughed self-consciously at her fervent words. "He really will, Pip," she said in her normal voice.

As they walked, Libby told Pip and Clay all that Chuck and the others in the Johnson family had done for her. "They prayed me into their family," she said after her story was finished. "I'm not always very nice, but they keep loving me and taking care of me anyway."

"I want a family just like that!" cried Pip.

"Dad always says Jesus makes the difference," said Susan.

"I want to know more about Jesus," said Pip.

"Me, too," said Clay.

Libby and Susan told Pip and Clay about Jesus. They walked slower and slower until finally they stopped right in the middle of the dirt road. The moon shone brightly and the sky was covered with stars.

"Will you help me pray for Jesus to be my Savior right now?" asked Pip softly.

"Me, too," said Clay.

"Sure," said Susan.

Smiling, Libby listened as Susan helped Pip and Clay pray. Libby remembered when she'd asked Jesus to be her Savior. She'd felt as if a great dark cloud had lifted off her. Chuck had told her that when she'd prayed, the real Libby, the Libby inside her, had become a whole new person. She heard Susan tell Pip and Clay the same thing.

Just then another flash of headlights cut through the darkness. Libby and the others ducked off the dirt road and hid in the safety of the trees.

"You know," said Pip in the sudden silence after the car disappeared from view. "This has been an amazing time, hasn't it? I'm glad now that you got stranded on the island."

"Me, too," said Susan.

Clay chuckled. "It would've been a lot easier if we could've become friends and learned about Jesus without being stranded."

"You're right," said Libby, laughing as she led the way back to the road. Suddenly she stopped. "Look up there! I see lights! House lights, I think. See them?"

"I do!" they all cried at once.

"Let's go!" said Libby, running a few steps. She stumbled and almost fell, then laughed. "I guess we'd better walk."

Several minutes later Libby was close enough that she could see it wasn't a house, but a small gas

station. A pay phone stood in plain view with a light shining over it. "We made it," said Libby happily.

Suddenly Clay caught her arm and pulled her up short. "Wait," he said, before she could run into sight of the lights. "Look!"

Pip gasped and Susan shivered.

Libby crept with the others behind some bushes and peeked out as two police cars stopped near the pay phone. Her heart almost stopped when they looked her way. Could they see them hiding? Would they flash their bright lights at them and grab them all?

She watched the officers get out of their cars and walk toward each other. They stopped near the phone and talked to each other. The drone of their voices drifted to Libby, but she couldn't make out what they were saying. Then one of them raised his voice.

"If those kids were around here, we'd have found them by now," he said. "Tomorrow morning when they drag the lake they'll probably find their bodies. I don't like it any better than you, but that's the way I see it!"

The other officer said something, shook his head, and walked back to his car. Finally he drove away.

The remaining officer walked into the run-down store and stayed several minutes. When he walked out, he was drinking pop from a can. He stood beside his car and looked right at where Libby and the others were hiding.

Libby trembled. Could he see them? Her mouth felt dry as she locked her icy hands together.

FOURTEEN
Rescued

Libby let out a long sigh of relief as the police car pulled away from the gas station. In the silence that followed she was sure the others could hear the wild beat of her heart.

"He's heading for the highway," said Clay hoarsely.

"I thought he saw us," said Pip, shivering. "But he didn't!"

"Let's go call," said Susan, taking a step forward.

"Wait!" Clay caught Susan's arm and tugged her back. "It would be better if only one person goes to the phone and makes the call in case someone drives up."

"Good idea," said Pip.

"I'll call," said Libby. She searched her pockets for money, but remembered she'd used her dollar to pay for the apples. "Anyone got any change?"

"I do," said Susan as she handed the money to Libby.

Libby closed her hand over the coins, took a deep breath, and walked to the pay phone. The bright light hurt her eyes for a minute. Bugs flew around the light and one dropped down to land in her tangled

hair. Shuddering, she brushed it away. Her hand
shook as she lifted down the receiver, dropped in the
coins, and called the Johnson farm.

Libby's legs grew weak when she heard Vera's voice
on the other end.

"Mom. It's Libby," she said, close to tears.

"Libby! Thank God you're safe! Where are you? Is
Susan with you? And the boy, Clay?"

"Yes," Libby told Vera where they were. "I don't
know the address, though."

"That's all right. I'm sure Chuck can find it. Just
sit tight. He'll be there in a short time. He's already
at the park and said he'd stay there looking until
he found you. He calls home every few minutes in
case one of you calls. Oh, Libby! I'm so glad you're
safe! I love you, honey. Tell Susan I love her and am
glad she's all right! And when you get home I want
to hear the whole story! Oh, Libby, I love you!"

"I love you, Mom." Reluctantly Libby hung up,
then ran back to the others and told them what Vera
had said.

Susan brushed away a tear. "I will not cry! Not
even happy tears," she said, brushing away another
tear.

Several minutes later Libby saw Chuck drive up
in his station wagon. She waited to make sure he was
alone, then they ran toward the car.

He heard them and ran to meet them. He gathered
Libby and Susan to him, tears slipping down his
cheeks. Finally he lifted his head, brushed away his
tears and said, "Thank God you're safe!"

"Dad, this is Clay and this is Pip," said Susan.

"Hello. I know about Clay, but not you, Pip,"

Chuck said. Suddenly he frowned. "Wait! I *do* know who you are!"

Pip gasped and turned away, but Susan caught her hand and held on tight.

Libby moved closer to Pip's other side in case she decided to run.

"Dad," said Susan. "Pip needs your help. I said you'd help her."

"I heard the news report," said Chuck slowly. "I think it would be better if we just drop Pip off at the police station."

"No!" cried Susan and Libby at once.

"I told you," whispered Pip hoarsely.

"A promise is a promise, Mr. Johnson," Clay said, squaring his thin shoulders. "Libby and Susan promised Pip you'd help her."

Chuck looked at Clay and then smiled. "Well, you're right. Jump in the car, Pip. I want to hear your story before I make a decision. I'm sure there must be more to your story than I heard on the news."

"There is," said Pip with a solemn nod.

Chuck hugged Clay to him. "We'll get you home. I told my wife to let your parents know that you're safe and on your way home."

"Thanks," said Clay, smiling up at Chuck. "Libby and Susan told us all about you, but they didn't say you had red hair. So does my dad."

Chuck looked at all of them and shook his head and smiled. "I prayed for you kids. I was very worried. But I knew God would keep you safe. He is a miracle worker."

"We found that out," said Pip.

"Yes," said Clay, breathing deeply.

Libby slipped in the back seat with Pip and Susan

while Clay sat up front with Chuck. The smell of the car was so familiar that Libby almost burst into tears. She saw the gum wrapper that Toby had dropped on the floor and forgot to pick up.

As Chuck drove, the kids filled him in on Pip's story. He nodded his head several times and asked questions occasionally. After they finished the story, he spent a few minutes thinking about the situation. Finally he said, "I think we should go to the police station. The Chief of Police is a friend of mine. We should let him know that you kids got back safely, and also that we found Pip."

"But they'll send her back to the detention home!" cried Libby. "We can't let that happen to her!"

Chuck sighed. "From what you're telling me, the police don't know the real story. If Pip went in and told Chief Edwards what you just told me, maybe they'd reconsider her placement in the home. Would you be willing to tell your story to the Chief, Pip?"

"I guess it's worth a try," she replied. She didn't sound very hopeful.

Everyone was silent as they drove to the police station. Libby was worried about Pip. What would happen to her now? She had thought for sure that Chuck would let Pip stay with them until her brother came to get her. But instead they were going to the police station. The police just *had* to help Pip stay with her brother!

Chuck pulled into the parking lot of the station. "Why don't you three stay in the car while Pip and I talk to Chief Edwards," he said, looking at Clay, Susan, and Libby. Libby gave Pip an encouraging smile as she left with Chuck.

Clay, Susan, and Libby didn't speak after they left. They were all thinking about Pip. After waiting almost half an hour, Chuck returned to the car. Pip wasn't with him.

"Where's Pip?" asked Susan anxiously.

"An officer will take her back to the home," Chuck said quietly.

"What?" exclaimed Clay, Susan and Libby at the same time. "I thought you would help her." said Libby.

"I did the best I could," replied Chuck. "But she must return to the home for now. I can't just take her away."

Then Chuck brightened. "Chief Edwards *did* listen to her story, though, and he agreed that her case should be presented in court again, this time without her dad's lies. The chief will contact a lawyer first thing tomorrow morning. Pip has a good chance to end up in legal custody of her brother."

"I wish we could do something for her," said Clay, a little disappointed at the outcome of the situation.

"We could pray for her," Libby suggested softly.

"That would help a lot," replied Chuck, smiling at Libby.

Several minutes later Chuck stopped outside Clay's house.

Libby said, "See you in school tomorrow, Clay."

"See you." He smiled at her. "Anytime you want a partner, ask for me."

"I sure will," she said. "And you do the same."

"I will." He lifted his hand and grinned.

"Bye, Susan. Let me know how everything turns out." He walked to his door with Chuck beside him.

The door burst open and his parents scooped him

into their arms. They talked to Chuck for a minute, then walked inside.

Much later, Libby was lying in bed with the sheet pulled to her chin. The door opened and Chuck walked in. He still wore his dark grey dress pants and light green shirt. She sat up as he sat on the edge of the bed.

"This has been quite a day, hasn't it, Elizabeth?" said Chuck.

She nodded. "I'm so glad we're home!"

"So am I!"

Libby hugged her knees to her chest. "I love you, Dad!"

"I love you, Elizabeth!"

In a low, halting voice she told him that she'd thought he'd stopped loving her. "But I know it's not true."

"Elizabeth, you're in my heart forever," he said as he gathered her close in his strong arms. She smelled his after-shave as she wrapped her arms tightly around him. She felt his heart thud against her. Finally he held her from him and looked into her face. "Elizabeth, God put a special love for you in my heart and nothing will ever take it away."

"I'm glad," she whispered.

He tucked her in and kissed her good night. "See you in the morning, my precious Elizabeth Gail."

"In the morning, Dad." She smiled and he smiled back, then she sat up and hugged him hard again.

After he tucked her in again, she watched him walk to the door, click off the light and walk out. Libby sighed heavily. Silently she prayed that Pip would know such love.

FIFTEEN
The news

Libby looked up from practicing her piano to see
Chuck and Clay walk in. She jumped up with a glad
cry. "Hi, Clay!"

"Surprise!" he said, grinning.

"I have news that I knew Clay would want to hear,
so I picked him up and brought him over," said Chuck.

"What's the news?" asked Libby.

"When the others come in I'll tell you," said Chuck.

"He wouldn't even give me a hint," said Clay, grinning as he sat on the piano bench beside Libby.

The others ran in, all talking at once. As soon as
they were seated Chuck said, "I have news about Pip."

Libby shivered and waited, her hands locked in
her lap.

"Just today Pip was officially put in her brother
Rusty's custody," said Chuck.

When the glad cheers stopped, Chuck continued.
"Pip's dad has agreed to family counseling. So once a
week, Pip, Rusty, and their dad meet with a coun-
selor. When I talked to Pip she said she thinks that

her dad will someday realize that he can love her and Rusty. They have a lot to work through, but Pip says with God's help they'll make it."

"That is *so* great!" cried Libby.

"I'm so happy I could cry," said Susan.

"And there's more," said Chuck, smiling.

"What else?" asked Clay, on the edge of his seat.

"You told me about Pip's friend Cindy. Well, Cindy is now living with wonderful foster parents who love her. I know them well. They're fine Christians and she's very happy with them. Plus, she and Pip get to see each other often."

A bubble of joy burst inside Libby as she cheered along with her family and Clay. Then she whispered, "Thank you, heavenly Father, for helping Pip find the love she needed."

ABOUT THE AUTHOR

Hilda Stahl was born and raised in the Nebraska Sandhills. When she was a young teen she realized she needed a personal relationship with God, so she accepted Christ into her life. She attended a Bible college where she met her husband, Norman. They and their seven children now live in Michigan.

When Hilda was a young mother with three children, she saw an ad in a magazine for a correspondence course in writing. She took the test, passed it, and soon fell in love with being a writer. She would write whenever she had free time, and she eventually began to sell what she wrote.

Hilda now has books with Tyndale House Publishers (the Elizabeth Gail series, The Tina series, The Teddy Jo series, and the Tyler Twins series), Accent Books (the Wren House mystery series), Bethel Publishing (the Amber Ainslie detective series, and *Gently Touch Sheela Jenkins*, a book for adults on child abuse), and Crossway Books (the Super JAM series for boys and *Sadie Rose and the Daring Escape*, for which she won the 1989 Angel Award). Hilda also has had hundreds of short stories published and has written a radio script for the Children's Bible Hour.

Some of Hilda's books have been translated into foreign languages, including Dutch, Chinese, and Hebrew. And when her first Elizabeth Gail book, *The Mystery at the Johnson Farm*, was made into a movie in 1989, it was a real dream come true for Hilda. She wants her books and their message of God's love and power to reach and help people all over the world. Hilda's writing centers on the truth that no matter what we may experience or face in life, Christ is always the answer.

Hilda speaks on writing at schools and organizations, and she is an instructor for the Institute of Children's Literature. She continues to write, teach, and speak—but mostly to write, because that is what she feels God has called her to do.

*If you've enjoyed the **Elizabeth Gail** series,
double your fun with these delightful heroines!*

Anika Scott

#1 The Impossible Lisa Barnes

#2 Tianna the Terrible

Cassie Perkins

#1 No More Broken Promises

#2 A Forever Friend

#3 A Basket of Roses

#4 A Dream to Cherish

#5 The Much-Adored Sandy Shore

#6 Love Burning Bright